CJ ALEXANDER

Into the Open

An alternative love story

First published by INDEPENDENT PUBLISHING 2022

First edition

ISBN: 9798797971504

Editing by Rhonda Merwath
Proofreading by April Grace O'Sullivan

This book was professionally typeset on Reedsy.
Find out more at reedsy.com

To my mum,
who taught me to love
wholeheartedly and unconditionally,
fiercely and fearlessly.

"We all straddle two fundamental
human needs:
the need for security,
and the need for adventure."

Esther Perel

Foreword

Six years ago, I decided to open up my relationship with my then-boyfriend to get our sexual needs met in a long-distance, cross-continental relationship. At the time, the alternatives – feeling sexually frustrated and resentful from being so far apart, going behind each other's backs to cheat, or breaking up – were equally unattractive options, and so non-monogamy was a decision that simply made logical and practical sense. However, we went about it with zero research and preparation, and generally had absolutely no idea what we were doing. My thirst for adventure and variety led to some impulsive and inconsiderate decision-making, and his insecurities and toxic masculine upbringing brought out unhealthy levels of jealousy and controlling, possessive behaviour. Neither of us knew of any resources to manage or process any of what we were experiencing, nor did we have any decent representation in the media of similar dynamics to give us a societal script to model ourselves after. Predictably, the relationship went down in flames a year later.

After the breakup, I dove into researching the world of non-monogamy and polyamory: reading books and blogs, listening to podcasts, and engaging in discussions on various online forums. As disastrous as my first experience was, I was confident that an open relationship was what I wanted and aligned with my core values. After a few more blunders here and there, I am now in a healthy polyamorous dynamic of several years, with a nesting partner I am building a life with, and multiple lovers dotted across the country. With every year that passes, more and more people are realising that monogamy is not the only option and are exploring other paths to relationship happiness. The COVID-19 crisis has also led many people to question their choices and identity; the famous Belgian psychotherapist Esther Perel once referred to "the erotic as an antidote to death" and this rings particularly true as I've noticed many people around me experiencing a fear of missing out. Perhaps being surrounded by so much tragedy makes people wonder if there is more to experience in their lifetimes while they still can.

These days, couples opening up their relationships are far more equipped to handle this monumental change to their dynamic with a wealth of content in all kinds of formats available for them to consume. Even if you don't personally desire multiple partners, the advice and insights within the polyamorous community are universally applicable to improving the health of your relationships with everyone you meet, not just your romantic partners. Being non-monogamous has helped me grow more as a person than anything else in my life, and is easily the best decision I have ever made.

Love and commitment have always meant so much more to me than simply refraining from falling in love with or having sex with other people. Polyamory has taught me about communication, intimacy, trust, respect, and communication in truly revolutionary ways.

While media representation of non-monogamous relationships still has a long way to go, open relationships are definitely part of the cultural zeitgeist in a way they were not at the beginning of my journey, and this book is part of that societal shift. This book will take you through so many different paths of self-discovery through connection, as well as the raw and realistic portrayal of the emotional struggles of opening up. The characters are on a difficult journey, but emerge on the other side as better people who have learned valuable lessons. Stories like this give me great hope for the future of polyamorous representation, and I hope you enjoy it as much as I did.

Leanne Yau,

Founder of the Poly Philia blog

Chapter 1

"**H**eads up!"

The warning comes just in time to watch the ball falling in slow motion toward my birthday cake, but—despite my flailing best efforts—not quite in time to actually move the cake before it's demolished before my very eyes. My mouth opens in an O of surprise as tiny shards of desiccated coconut snow down all around us, a large glob of icing hitting the right eye of my brand-new sunglasses. I don't know whether to laugh or cry. It must have been an accident (I can't believe anyone could ever manage to hit a cake that perfectly on purpose?) so I need to calm down or I'll make a fool of myself. I take a deep breath.

The boy comes over to collect his ball, wearing a sheepish look.

After doing his best to remove the worst of the cake, Jonathan stands up to pass the ball back to him.

"I'm so sorry," the boy mumbles in a tiny voice, staring down at his feet.

"Honestly, it's fine. We're stuffed anyway. You've just helped us with our diet!" Jonathan tells him jubilantly as the boy gazes up to him with a relieved smile.

He grabs the ball and dashes off to the safety of his mates, who are laughing and jeering, clearly eager to find out what happened. The group quietens as they realise he didn't get in trouble, and they're back to their game of football in no time.

"I'm so sorry. You've put all this effort in, and it's ruined now," I say to Jonathan as I ineffectually attempt to wipe my sunglasses clean, smearing icing across them in the process.

"Don't be silly. It's not like you've never tried this cake before, is it?" Jonathan says, laughing. He's bought me this exact same cheap cake from the Co-op for every birthday I've had since I was eighteen, decorated with sweets to show my ever-increasing years. He receives the chocolate version on his own birthday.

The interruption has burst our happy picnic bubble, and the park comes to life around me: sounds of children playing, young ones with their parents feeding the ducks; clusters of teenagers sitting around chatting; and the boy and his friends having a kickabout between jumper-marked goals. Jonathan is focused on doing his best to clean up and salvage what he can of the cake.

"When did it get so busy all of a sudden? There was no one here when we arrived!"

"School has finished for the day now," replies Jonathan, watching the game of football. "I reckon they must be some of the new year sevens; he was a bit too small for his uniform, wasn't he?"

When you and your parents are all teachers, you must have a genetically programmed eye for spotting these things. Now that I look at the boys properly, I can see he's probably right. They all seem a bit shellshocked—enjoying, but perhaps also a little scared of, their new freedom. Those early high school days are long forgotten for me, but I do remember starting Sixth Form and feeling the same, with the freedom of suddenly being able to wear our own clothes to school. We felt so grown up back then, but we weren't quite ready for it, that awkward in-between stage, preparing for both the best and worst days of your life. Not that I feel ready now, though, even at the ripe old age of twenty-four. Twenty-four! My mum had already had my brother Tom and was pregnant with me by this age.

"Jonathan, I'm bored," I blurt out.

He stares at me, with pieces of squashed cake from the picnic he's lovingly prepared for me on his fingers, a look of confusion and despair. A squashed cake might not have ruined our picnic, but apparently I'm going to. This isn't how this conversation was supposed to go. I start pulling at the smooth grass, stretching it out and wrapping it around my fingers, unable to meet his eye.

I can't say something like that and not follow it up with some kind of explanation, though. I take a breath and close my eyes for a second to steel myself before looking up at him. This is it. I've started something now and I need to run with it. "I mean, not right now. I'm having a lovely time, thank you. I've had such a great birthday and the picnic has been perfect, even with the ruined cake and everything, and I know how hard it must've been for you to get away from school so early. I really appreciate it. I...just... I see those kids and it reminds me of us back in Sixth Form with all our plans and ideas, excited about the future, but I've not really done anything, have I? I love you and I love our house, and you're working so hard to make it nice for us. And I even like work most of the time—I don't hate it at least. I'm just a bit bored. Everything is so predictable. What if this is it? Nothing changes from how we are now except we get

3

older? Doesn't it feel boring to you? Where's the excitement, the adventure? What's the point?"

I'm rambling, making it worse. I've been having these thoughts for a while now, planning this speech in my head, but I've got terrible timing; he's gone to all this effort to make today special, and this is how I repay him? I feel so ungrateful, and I don't know how to fix it. If I thought the boys looked shellshocked, that was nothing compared to his expression now. He's utterly speechless; I can see him trying and failing to form words. He wasn't prepared for this. I can feel my heart racing, beads of sweat forming on my forehead as I try to find a way to make it all better again.

We both fall silent. Jonathan is taking in what I've said whilst I'm in a nervous agony, biting my nails while awaiting some kind of response. To distract myself, I return to watching the children feeding the ducks nearby—two little girls beneath masses of gorgeous twisty hair, dressed in matching dungarees and giggling together, seeing who can throw their seeds the farthest as the ducks squabble over their feast.

Their mum turns and she seems familiar, but I can't quite place her. She appears to be having the same thought process as she glances back at me with an uncertain smile before waving and walking toward us, to our rescue. "Sophie! How are you?" Her smile is wide now, full red lips framing perfect white teeth and brightening an otherwise quite stern face. She comes across as smart and serious, with her flawless black bob and her houndstooth jacket zipped up to her neck.

It's Lucy. We worked together when I was twenty and temping in a law firm. Lucy was one of their youngest and brightest solicitors. Everyone was disappointed when she left for her maternity leave—knowing she was having twins, they understood it was unlikely she'd return. Presumably they were right to think that, as she's here in the park feeding the ducks at four p.m. on a Thursday. We'd not mixed much when we worked together; there was a bit of an awkward divide between the legal professionals and the rest of us. At twenty, I certainly didn't feel good enough to try to bridge it. Apart from a couple of occasions like this, we haven't stayed in touch, but boy am I glad to see her now and escape this awkward silence with Jonathan.

Before I know it, Jonathan has introduced himself and is doing a dramatic retelling of the ball-in-the-cake story as we all tuck into the rest of the sweet strawberries. Everyone is smiling and laughing, and my awkward speech is forgotten for the moment at least.

Lucy's laughing like a drain at Jonathan's story, and I can see him puff up a bit, proud of himself for holding her attention like this. "It's your birthday! You must come out with us next weekend; we're having a girls' night out. It'd be lovely to catch up after all these years, hear what fun things you've been up to whilst I've been knee-deep in nappies."

We exchange numbers, knowing we'll never use them, and she takes the girls' hands and walks them over to the swings.

"You should call her, go out with her. It'd be nice for you to make some new friends, let off some steam," Jonathan suggests.

"She was just being polite because it's my birthday." Who's he to tell me what I should do? I have no intention whatsoever of going out on a mums' night out, hearing all about their darling children, endless nappy changes, useless husbands and PTA gossip, all peppered with their well-meaning questions about my biological clock. No, thank you.

5

* * *

Over the next few days as I go through my usual boring routine (get up, go to work, come home, eat dinner, watch TV, go to bed) I realise that maybe a night out and some new friends wouldn't be the worst idea. There's no point in me complaining I'm bored if I'm not going to do anything about it. I really should push myself a bit, get out of my comfort zone. What's the worst that can happen, anyway? A boring night listening to parents talking about their kids, and then I come home early? A hangover?

I decide I will get in touch with Lucy, and I will go on this girls' night out.

Chapter 2

"**M**orning, sunshine!" sings Jonathan's far-too-sprightly voice in the far-too-light room, far too early for me to bear, on the morning after my night out with Lucy.

"Go away," I reply, pulling the duvet over my head.

A rush of air hits my—oh God, still-tightly-squeezed-into-my-favourite-shocking-pink-dress—body, as Jonathan climbs back onto the bed next to me in his mucky painting clothes. "I made you breakfast," he whispers, his voice dripping with sarcastic sympathy.

With every ounce of energy I can muster, I pull myself up to a sitting position and see the tray. Steaming-hot tea. A pink smoothie. Linda McCartney sausages, mushrooms, and spicy slow-cooked beans on toast. It smells incredible, comforting, the answer to all my problems. Best of all, there are two beautiful white paracetamol pills, too. "I love you!" I exclaim, reaching for the pills and washing them down with half of the sweet-tasting smoothie, instantly transforming my hangover headache into an ice cream headache instead.

Jonathan watches in bemused silence as I devour my breakfast feast and then clamber out of bed, pulling off my clothes.

"How was your girly night?"

"It was okay. I hope I didn't wake you when I came in?"

"Not really."

I head to the bathroom, the smell of yesterday's fresh paint overpowering. Flushing the toilet, I take a look at myself in the mirror. Last night's mascara rings my eyes, making me appear even more pale and gaunt than usual. My overbleached hair creates a halo of frizz around my head and I wonder for a moment if I should cut myself a fringe. An enormous spot is brewing under my skin, right in the middle of my cheek. I splash my face with water and do my best to both wake up and remove my makeup all at once.

I take a breath and walk back to the bed, my pillow smudged with last night's makeup. "I met a guy," I say, attempting to sound casual.

"Oh, yeah?"

"He was nice. Javier. He's over here from Spain, studying English in Oxford for a year as part of his degree."

Those big, sweet, brown eyes look up at me expectantly, but hesitantly too. I pause, knowing this could be one of those life-defining moments that will haunt me forever. I want to stay in this comfortable safety a little longer.

"And, um...we kissed. It was nice."

A moment of silence as I watch him take this in, not quite knowing how he'll react. I can almost see it physically hit him and then him pushing it down, willing himself to accept what he's heard and be okay with it. I'm not entirely sure which way this is going to go, but I'm hopeful he will be okay. It was just a kiss, after all. I can feel the tension tight in every part of my body as I wait for him to respond.

"Let's get you in that shower, shall we?"

I guess that's the end of that conversation then. Do I take that to mean it's okay?

As I return from the shower, towel heavy on my head, my phone bleeps: a text from Lucy. *Hair of the dog?*

I think about it and realise I really did have fun last night. I like Lucy. It would be nice to have a new friend. And a pint certainly wouldn't hurt, either.

Chapter 3

"Sophie! Where did you get to last night, young lady?" booms Lucy's voice as she strides confidently into the pub two hours later, distracting me from finishing the half-written response to my mum's regular check-in text.

"I'm really sorry. I got tired and wanted to go home. It was too busy in there to find you to say goodbye. Sorry. Did you have a good night?"

She nods and smiles knowingly before heading to the bar. I take in this immaculate woman as she returns with a small white wine, plus a second pint of lager for me. There's no way she slept in her clothes last night or failed to take her makeup off. No matter what time or state she returns home in, she gets herself sorted properly, I know it. Her neat black bob is always perfect. Her dark red nails match her lipstick, which shows off her perfectly white teeth. How does she do it all with her kids running around, too? I'm in awe of her.

In contrast, after my shower this morning, I simply pulled on dirty joggers and a bright blue sweatshirt with *LUCKY* emblazoned across the chest in big white letters before scraping my wet-but-not-washed hair into a bun. I feel ridiculously underdressed and it's not helping my hangover one bit.

Plonking my pint down in front of me, before she's even fully sat down, she asks, "So what happened? You were talking to that guy for ages, and then you just disappeared. Everyone thinks you went home with him. Did you?"

Straight to the point, this one—no beating around the bush. Is this why she messaged me, just for gossip? I thought we'd got on last night and I really do want to be her friend. I look her in the eye whilst taking a moment to decide what I should say before landing on brutal honesty. She's not stupid; she'll end up getting the truth in the end, so I should just get on with it. This could make or break our friendship, but if it's going to break it, I might as well get it over with straight away before I am too invested. "I didn't go home with him. But we kissed."

She seems a bit shocked, perhaps more at my honesty than the kiss itself, which she clearly had her suspicions about already.

I don't pause for her to pass comment. Instead, I tell her this isn't the first time. I launch into my story and, when the dam bursts, there's no stopping me. I've kept this inside for too long. It feels good to get it out there at last, even to someone I hardly know. I have no idea how she's going to react, but it's too late to worry about that now.

Telling the story to Lucy, it's almost like I'm back there, six months ago, squished into that tiny three-door Kia Rio with four almost-strangers after a hen night in Brighton. My head bouncing on the blissfully cold window, occasional breaks to allow a big whoosh of air in to revive us all a little, or at least wake us with that awful thump-thump-thump of an open window on a motorway. A five-hour drive in blazing sunshine, all of us feeling worse for wear but trying our best to make small talk, not knowing each other well enough to just sit in comfortable sleepy silence.

I'd been lost in hazy memories of the previous night. They'd all seen me kiss a stranger. Not a silly hen night dare, but a proper gropey snog. Everyone knew about Jonathan, because I'd been going on and on all day about how wonderful he was. And they'd be meeting him a month later at their wedding. That meant I had no choice but to tell him or live in fear for the whole of their wedding day—and no doubt the rest of eternity—that one of them would say something.

"That kiss was magical," I tell Lucy, coming out of my reverie. "It was as if time had stopped, as if we were the only people in the world. He was hypnotising, hanging on to my every word, making me feel beautiful, funny and interesting. It was the same feeling last night, too. I wish I didn't need that external validation to feel good, but it does feel good, and I like it. I know Jonathan loves me, and I love him too, but it was just so nice to feel wanted like that for once. Our kisses aren't magical or time-stopping anymore, ever."

Daft Punk's "Get Lucky" was the appropriate soundtrack to our kiss, and I still think of that first guy when I hear it now, just like I'll think of last night every time I hear Katy Perry sing about the eye of the tiger—she empowered me to take what I wanted.

"The overriding feeling I had whilst rumbling along in that car back from Brighton was excitement," I continue. "I was honestly looking forward to telling Jonathan. I was so anxious to get it over with and find out one way or another how he was going to react, rather than sitting in that blazing-hot car, imagining a thousand possible scenarios, each worse than the last."

Lucy seems suitably worried at this point, her head tilted

to the side as she gawps at me with wide eyes, the whites bright and shiny against the darkness of her pupils and skin. I've definitely caught her interest now; she looks enthralled, even though she knows he can't have reacted too badly or we wouldn't still be together. She's leaning toward me and it's a similar feeling to the kiss—I've grasped her full, undivided attention all for myself.

I sit a little taller, feeling powerful and interesting. "I don't know what I'd really expected him to say when I told him, but I certainly wasn't picturing his calm and measured response. There was no argument, no shouting. He just accepted what I'd told him and that I still loved him and wanted to be with him. Our sex life had a massive boost; we went from me initiating all the time and getting turned down to him wanting it more than I did. No more was said about the kiss, though, even at the wedding. It was like he'd accepted it as a one-time thing that shocked him into bucking his ideas up."

I see her shoulders relax as she breathes out in relief, but there's more to tell yet.

"A couple of months later, he was off to Prague on a stag do, and I made it clear I wouldn't mind if he had some fun whilst he was out there. Not wanting to waste such an offer, he took full advantage and kissed a girl. He rang me at two a.m. to tell me about it, all proud of himself!"

Lucy looks at me, eyes wide. This wasn't the conversation she'd been expecting to have today. She's happily married, living in a nice detached house, complete with a garage and garden, in the suburbs with her twin four-year-old girls Hannah and Freya. This isn't her world. What must she think of me?

But I still don't let her comment. There's still more to tell, and I'm really in my stride now. "When he got back from Prague, I wanted to know *everything*. What was she like? Where was she from? Did he get her number? Did he have a picture? Where did they meet? What happened? Did any of his friends see? What did they say? I was an endless barrage of questions. He was hungover and tired, so could barely keep up with me. But I kept asking, and the more he told me, the more attractive he became. This hot, interesting guy who could still pull a gorgeous girl on a night out wasn't the same boring old Jonathan who'd left just days before. I saw him in a whole new light and wanted him more than ever."

Later that night, we'd had the most incredible sex after he'd described what it was like kissing her, what he'd have liked to do with her, and what he'd have done if he could have got me and her in a room together. It was the first time I ever squirted, my body completely giving itself over to pleasure—thinking about having sex with someone else, with a girl, and being watched. That's still probably the best sex we've ever had together, but Lucy doesn't need to hear about that right now.

Sparing her my sex stories, instead I go on to explain the months of conversations that followed. How our desires were reignited: after years together doing the same old thing, we suddenly saw each other anew and realised we might lose what we had and couldn't take each other for granted.

Although I'd been completely besotted with Jonathan since the day we'd met, I'd always had crushes on other people, too. I'd thought there was something wrong with me, that I couldn't really be as in love as I thought I was if I was thinking about other people, so I tried to ignore my feelings. But now I've kissed two other people and I know I still love Jonathan. He's kissed someone else, and I'm sure he still loves me. It has to be possible to make this work.

I go on to explain to Lucy that eventually we'd decided to give this whole monogamish, open, polyamorous, whatever-you-want-to-call-it thing a go and see where it led us. We made long lists of rules, constantly editing and adding to them the more we talked. Eventually we agreed we wouldn't actively seek out other partners, but if opportunities came along, we could still take them and enjoy them.

So last night was the first time. The first time either of us kissed someone else with a sort-of prior approval, without having to worry about telling each other the next day. I know I've done nothing wrong, but I still need to work out exactly how Jonathan feels about this development.

As I come to the end of my tale, Lucy looks at me and smiles. "Good for you!"

The relief of finally telling someone, and having her react positively, is incredible. I feel about a stone lighter, my hangover forgotten.

And then comes the phrase I know I'm going to become so familiar with over the coming months: "I don't think I could do it myself, but it sounds really exciting for you." Finally, a concerned expression takes over as she leans in closer to me, her eyebrows slightly furrowed, and quietly follows up with a question. "And you're sure, really sure, that Jonathan's okay with all this?"

With this question, I know I made a good decision confiding in Lucy. She's briefly met Jonathan once, so she has no real reason to care how he feels, but she still does anyway. She's a good person, not just here for gossip after all. I'm relieved.

Chapter 4

Returning home, Lucy's question burns in my ears. *Is Jonathan okay? Really okay?* Her concern has piqued mine, and now I'm anxious to get home to him as fast as I can.

I crash urgently through the front door, eager to see him and reconnect. But he's not here. Not in the lounge, where he should be finishing off painting. Not in the kitchen. Not in the bath or on the toilet. Not in bed. Not. Here.

I'm pacing now, my heart racing with my panic. Where the fuck is he? Doesn't he know how much I need to see him right now? He never goes out. Where has he gone? Why now? When will he be back? Has he gone forever? Shit! What have I done?

I feel like I should apologise for the kiss, promise I'll never do it again. That's what people do in this situation, right? But I can't, I won't. I'm not sorry, and I don't want to make a promise I don't think I can keep.

I text him: *Where are you?*

But no matter how often I check, he doesn't respond.

I decide to text my best friend Amy, not quite knowing what I want to say. I go with a simple cheery, *How are you?* to which I also receive no response.

Hours later, I wake up on the sofa with dribble running down my cheek, mascara down my face once again, throat dry and metallic-tasting, TV blaring. It's dark. Sitting up, I spot Jonathan in the armchair—he must've woken me when he came in. That, or he's been sitting there watching me sleep for God knows how long. I can't work out his expression, but he seems stressed, his chestnut hair dishevelled and brown eyes red-rimmed.

"Hey," I croak.

"Hey."

"How are you? How are we?"

He looks at me with so much love that tears start to swell behind my eyes, a lump forming in my throat. "We're okay. It was a bit of a shock. I needed some space to take it all in. But you've done nothing wrong. We agreed to do this. I guess maybe I thought I'd be first or something."

"I'm sorry."

And I am sorry. Not for the kiss itself, but for hurting him like this.

"Don't be sorry. It's okay. Just a little harder than I expected it would be. I bumped into Chris, and he said I should finish with you, but it's not that simple. It helped me see clearly, though—I want to be with you. I do want to make this work for us."

Chris! Of all the people he could've spoken to, Chris is far from my first choice. He was at school with Jonathan and is now married to a gossipy woman I can hardly bear to spend time with, let alone worry that she knows my secrets. But I'm glad he has spoken to someone, and I'm really glad it's helped him realise he wants to be with me. And he certainly knows and trusts Chris more than I do Lucy.

He comes over and snuggles awkwardly in with me on the sofa, a positive sign. I manoeuvre myself into a more comfortable position and gaze up into his eyes.

"I love you so much," I say, gently kissing the end of his nose.

"You too."

"Do you want to talk about it? Ask me anything?"

One look tells me that is a definite *no*.

I want to ask a million questions: what does this mean for us? What will happen next? I'm scared he'll say it's too hard and he can't cope with the feelings this brings up, that this is all going to be over before it's even begun. Chatting to and kissing Javier last night made me feel alive, funny, and sexy. Just the sound of his voice was alluring, the way his name formed on his lips as he helped me pronounce it properly—*Hav-ee-air*—after my appalling first few attempts. We both had to listen attentively to understand each other's accents over the sound of the music, but no matter how interesting what he was telling me was, I was always half distracted by the thought of kissing him. The anticipation of what might happen next was addictive. I realise now that I'm not ready to stop this.

I want to fall madly in love with someone, the passionate, exciting way songs and films tell me about, the way Jonathan assures me only happens in songs and films and is unrealistic. But how can it be? All those writers must've experienced those things. It's not all fantasy.

I want the lust, anticipation, desire, frustration, and even the heartbreak. I want to be with an older guy who will look after me and make me feel like a princess. I want to be with a younger guy I can look after and become the wise and experienced one. I want to be open to every opportunity that might come my way, to decide if I want to do something for myself, rather than having to think more about the impact it might have on Jonathan than whether I want it or not. I want to spend all of Sunday in bed, lazing around, sleeping, kissing, cuddling, talking, having sex, eating and drinking without a care in the world, no stupid DIY or worrying about stacks of schoolbooks needing to be marked. I want it all.

Why should I have to forgo those experiences because I found a deep and lasting love with Jonathan when I was young? I don't want to give that up for something I know will be fun, but ultimately less fulfilling, but I do still want to have all that too. Am I being greedy and selfish, wanting to have my cake and eat it too? That's what people will think, isn't it? I don't think what I want is so strange, really, just that no one admits it. Do I really want to be the person who does? The person who has to face other people's judgements and comments? Am I brave enough to stick up for myself like that?

But, as scary as it all is, I really *do* want this. It's tugging away inside me, consuming my thoughts. I can't ignore it.

I build up my nerve and say what's really on my mind, "The thing is... The thing is, I got his number. And I'd like to see him again."

Jonathan seems to flinch at this. A random, one-off kiss with a stranger is one thing. A planned date—and the things it might lead to—is quite another.

"I need some time and space to think about this, please."

I can't argue with that.

Chapter 5

"Sophie, will you go and serve table four now, please?" whisper-shouts Julie.

I've drifted off into a daydream at the coffee machine again, thinking about what it would be like to have sex with Javier, or anyone who isn't Jonathan, discovering a new body and all of its secrets for the first time, and not to mention the idea of having someone else discover mine. I'm also imagining ways I could show Jonathan I love him and that he should trust me and let me do this.

The bell tinkles as an elderly couple comes into the café, rosy-cheeked and with matching candyfloss hair dishevelled by the wind outside. He holds the door open for her, takes her hand to walk the few metres to their table, pulls out her chair and takes her coat. What a gentleman! They seem so happy and so in love, infectious peals of unashamed laughter coming from their table every few minutes. They seem more solid somehow than many of our elderly customers, who are usually sweet and smiley too, but look like they might blow away if the wind becomes too strong. I watch them for a while as I wonder whether Jonathan and I will make it through this, if we'll ever get to be that old and still be so devoted to each other.

"Sophie! Table four!" Julie repeats, springing me into action.

I've been distracted like this for weeks now, trying to give Jonathan time and space to think about all this. My head is full of memories of the kiss and what it would be like to see Javier again, kiss him again, be naked with him, and to feel his hands and his tongue on my skin. It's all I can think about. I'm desperate to text him and see if he's interested, worried that if I don't do it soon, I'll be too late. It might even be too late already. I'm trying so hard to respect what Jonathan has asked for, to go at his pace, but I'm impatient and frustrated with it.

After work, slumped on the sofa watching *The Simpsons* over a big bowl of pasta, I try to broach the subject again. "Have you given any more thought to what we talked about?"

"What?"

"About me wanting to see that guy again."

"Oh. No, I haven't had a chance."

He hasn't had a chance! Can't he see how important this is to me? Surely if it bothers him so much, it should be all he can think about too? I've given him time and space specifically for this, and he's chosen not to take it. I'm livid, my hands squeezed into involuntary fists, my breathing heavy. But showing him this isn't going to get me anywhere.

I take a deep breath. "Okay. Do you think you could make some time to think about it? Please?" *Like now, instead of wasting time watching TV repeats you've seen a thousand times*, I add silently, straining from the effort to stop my eyes from rolling in my head.

I storm off, my nostrils flaring and jaw tight. I can't let him see me like this; he thinks he's the one who's hard done by here, the one who should be feeling angry, and most people would probably agree I'm the unreasonable one.

More weeks pass uneventfully; it's torturous for me. I keep making attempts to talk, but he just keeps shutting me down, always too busy doing some DIY job around the house (the smell of fresh paint constant and overpowering, the sound of drilling and hammering giving me a permanent headache) or planning lessons and marking homework. I shouldn't complain. I want our house to be finished, and it's great that he's working so hard on it, and I love that he's passionate about his job, but I'd rather have some proper time together. We are having sex, but not like after his Prague experience when it was mind-blowing—we are just back to our old ways. I'm bored. So fucking bored. I've given up hope of seeing Javier again; even if Jonathan gave his blessing, too much time has passed now.

I've not heard from Amy at all. She must've found herself a new boyfriend. But I've seen Lucy a couple more times for a drink; it's been fun getting to know her better, and we always laugh a lot. With her girls to look after, I don't think she manages to get out much, so she likes that if she finds herself with a bit of spare time, she can contact me and I'm usually free. Most of her other friends seem to have children too, so she doesn't even try them anymore. The advantages of having a friend who's childless and lonely!

I join Lucy and her girls for Bonfire Night, all of us wrapped up in coats and hats so we can stay out for as long as possible without getting too close to the fire. Lucy is adorable and cosy in her big fluffy scarf, a cuddle personified. Jonathan stays at home with a stack of marking to get through, and I'm still yet to meet her husband, Dave.

Hannah and Freya are happily tucking into a pair of toffee apples, red sugar all over their faces, little crystals on their gloves glinting red in the firelight like the lights in the heels of their light-up trainers. The smell of slightly over-ripe apples mixed with the sugar is sickly.

"Any goss?" Lucy asks me, half an eye on her girls who are watching the fire, clearly mesmerised. After the excitement of my tales when we went for that first drink together, I think I've left her feeling as disappointed as I am with my lack of dramatic updates since.

"Not really. I'm trying my best to be patient with Jonathan, giving him time to reflect and think. But I don't think he's using it to do that. He's choosing to forget about it all, burying his head in the sand. How about you, any exciting sexy stories to share?"

"Ha! Well, I can't even remember the last time I had sex, even with myself! I kind of lost interest after the girls were born. I was sore and tired; we'd just get one off to sleep and the other would wake up." She laughs at my poorly hidden horrified expression at the thought of those sleepless nights. "It wasn't so bad really, honestly. I was determined to breastfeed for as long as I could, so it was always me up with them, for six months straight. And I don't resent that. I'm proud of feeding them for as long as I did."

I can see the pride in her eyes as she tells me this. She's standing a little taller than normal. I feel proud of her. I may not know much about babies, but I do know I'm no fun to be around if I've not had my solid eight hours of sleep.

"Even if I'd had more energy back then, I certainly didn't want anyone else touching me after having the girls on me all day and night. They're four now, so we've had three and a half years to get back to it, but it just hasn't happened. We're stuck in a rut I suppose."

Where I could see her pride when she talked about breastfeeding her girls, I can't quite make out how she feels about this. I'm not sure if she's disappointed it's not happening or simply relieved, or perhaps a little uncomfortable and embarrassed to be talking about sex at all.

"I would be losing my mind! I don't know how you do it with your girls. I'd need the sex to help me chill out or just to get to sleep!"

"Getting to sleep isn't a problem for me after I've been chasing them around all day! Anyway, next year they'll be at school full time. Maybe things will change then. It doesn't bother me now, though. Secretly, I'm glad I don't have to do it. Is that awful?"

That relief is clearer now; she's smiling and her breathing seems deeper. I can't imagine ever being relieved to not have sex. I want it far more than Jonathan does. If anything, he'd be pleased if we did it a bit less—I just wish I could make him see that letting me do it with someone else might help both of us get what we need.

The fireworks begin, a display Guy Fawkes himself would be proud of. Lucy's girls run into her arms where they can safely enjoy the display without worrying about the big, loud noises in the dark. In moments like this, I can see the appeal of having children, of feeling so unconditionally loved and needed like that. I want to join in their lovely, cosy cuddle. It looks so happy and safe in there, the fireworks reflected in the girls' wide eyes. I find myself oohing and ahhing out loud for the first time in my life, something I used to cringe at my mum for doing when I was a child, but I can't stop myself now. Watching fireworks with children is an entirely magical experience. I pull out my phone and take a picture of the three of them, lit by the fire.

Chapter 6

E ventually, I can take it no more. I wake Jonathan with the smell of fresh coffee and breakfast in bed on Saturday morning. Once he's awake and fed, I take a breath and say my piece.

"I've decided I won't get in touch with Javier. But I have heard about an open relationship dating app. Do you want to give it a try, see if we can both find someone and get ourselves a date?" I'm talking too fast, uncertain of what he's going to say.

In contrast to my haste, he's taking too long to respond, avoiding eye contact with me. "I'm not sure I want a date. I just want you."

I can't help but feel warm and fuzzy at this; it's what every girl grows up dreaming of being told, even if it's getting in the way of what I really want. "I know you do, and it's so sweet of you. But aren't you just a little bit intrigued? To see if you match with anyone? To try going on a date where you've got nothing to lose? I've never even had a real date with anyone except you. I want to know what it's like!"

He goes quiet, but for once he seems to be seriously digesting what I've said, rather than avoiding it by trying to change the subject. I snuggle into his chest, feeling his soft skin and tickly hairs against my cheek, his sleepy smell familiar and comforting. "Okay. I'll try it. But I'm not promising anything. We can go on the app, but that doesn't mean I'm definitely going to be okay with either of us going on a date."

"That's fair enough. Shall we do it now then?"

"Right now? Can I at least get out of bed first?"

My excitement and impatience has got the better of me once again.

Equal footing seems to be more appealing than me rushing ahead on my own. Once he's up and dressed, we both download the app and help each other set up our profiles, even switching phones to choose photos and answer some of the questions.

I choose a picture of Jonathan sitting in the park this summer, the glow of a sunny day visibly shining out of him. He is so relaxed in it, enjoying the summer holidays, a break from teaching, from endless planning and marking. It's probably not the most flattering angle, but I can't help but smile every time I see it—it makes me feel almost as happy as he looks.

For my main photo, he chooses one of me from the summer too, in trainers and a pleated miniskirt with a crop top. I look young and carefree, more preppy than I usually do. I remember him taking it—we'd gone out for lunch and stayed in the beer garden all afternoon, laughing with each other. We don't have enough days like that, with nowhere to be, nothing to do. There's always DIY to be done, lessons to plan. I wish I could have his attention like that more often.

"So, what do we say we want here?" Jonathan's question makes this all a whole lot more real; we're finally talking about this seriously. I can feel the excitement bubbling up inside me,

26

the anticipation of what might be to come.

"I'm not sure. It'd be nice to see someone about once or twice a month, and do fun dates too, not just sex stuff. I don't like the idea of it just being sex; I want to be sure I actually get on with the person, too. I guess I want a friends-with-benefits kind of arrangement."

"Okay. I think that sounds better than just sex. I want to know they'll respect you and not do anything to you that I wouldn't."

That's a relief. I definitely don't want just sex, but I can see how adding something more meaningful could be difficult for some people to handle. I was especially nervous about discovering Jonathan's unease at answering that question. "And would you want to meet the person, go on dates together, or maybe try group sex?"

Jonathan is a little taken aback at this suggestion. "No! That's too much. I can just about get on board with the idea of you being with someone else, but I don't want to see it."

Finally we both settle on the same slightly vague but hope-fully intriguing description: *I'm in a happy long-term relation-ship, looking for some extra fun and friendship.*

It's exciting helping each other choose our best pictures and describe ourselves, but then we disappear off alone to explore. The first guy I swipe right on matches with me instantly, and it sets my heart racing. I feel completely validated, on top of the world; it's a real high.

I make eight more matches in an hour. Who knew so many hot guys were out there that would be interested in a girl like me? (On reflection: everyone, duh. I'm in a happy, committed relationship and seeking casual sex. They know I mean it when I say casual—Jonathan's profile is right there, attached to mine.

27

They know there's no risk I'll want to move in with them and start nagging them about washing up, or want to get married or have their babies. Casual means casual. What's not to like?)

Jonathan matches with no one. I'm not sure if he's being too picky or there just aren't that many girls on there, or if maybe it's something about his profile. I'm gutted, even more than he seems to be.

I start messaging some of my matches over the next few days. Friendly chat I can handle. It's nice: guys telling me I'm hot or pretty, asking about my life, telling me about their day. Some want to get into deep conversations, asking about my relationship setup or telling me about theirs, how their wife wants to open up but they're not sure. It's sort of interesting and nice to know it's not just me, but boring too; I have enough of those conversations with Jonathan, and it's not what I'm here for. Some do ask what I'm looking for, though, and I don't know how to answer. I'm not too sure exactly what I want yet. I need to explore it more. I know I feel like something is missing from my life, and the drunken kisses I've had seem to have gone some way towards finding it. I don't really know if I want sex or love or attention or even just friendship.

Some send my heart into a flutter when I see their name pop up. Others make me do an internal groan, and it's that and nothing else—not their pictures or the quality of the conversation—that tells me whether I should continue chatting with them. But turning down someone who's hot and nice to chat to just because my stomach doesn't flip at the mere sight of their name is incredibly empowering.

One, Ellis, tells me he's about to have a wank and asks if I want to watch. I'm not sure I do, but Jonathan is out so I'm home alone and might as well make the most of it. I say yes in the interests of sexual exploration and getting outside of my comfort zone, grabbing the opportunities that come my way.

I give him my number and get a video call almost immediately. On answering, I'm greeted not by his face, but by his hard, naked penis. A sharp intake of breath gives away my shock and I'm slightly ashamed of how unworldly I must seem to him. I am a little taken aback, but I've never done this before. Maybe it's normal? Perhaps he wants to protect his anonymity so I can't do a screenshot of his face or something? This feels more weird than sexy, but I've come this far so I want to see it through, to see if I have the guts to actually watch, and maybe even join in myself.

His hand starts stroking and after a moment's hesitation, I decide to just dive in. Having him watching me seems less frightening than having to attempt to talk dirty for him.

My heart is beating so hard with nerves, I feel sure he must be able to hear it. Nevertheless, I take off my top and show him my tits as my hand descends slowly into my pants. I still can't see his face, but I can hear appreciative noises and his breath becoming faster. A sudden groan pulls me into the moment, sending me from awkward and uncomfortable to horny just like that.

Knowing he's watching and turned on by me is explosive, my discomfort evaporating quickly. I'm wet, in the moment, and excited to play. I want to put on my best performance. I push my fingers into my increasingly wet pussy and rub my clit hard with my thumb, always keeping half an eye on my screen to check my open mouth and tits are in full view for him.

I move my hand to play with my nipple, licking my lips slowly. I receive more appreciative grunts as I do so. Hearing him losing control like that is so hot, and I find myself more in the moment and enjoying myself, finally putting my own pleasure first rather than just trying to put on a show for him.

I slide my hand back down my body. I move my fingers harder and faster around my wet cunt and I'm making more noise than usual. My face and chest are becoming more flushed. I can't remember the last time I didn't use a toy, but my fingers seem to remember what to do, and I shudder as I come loudly.

Almost as though he's been waiting for me to go first, the moment I'm done, he comes. And as he comes, I hold my phone to my wide-open mouth so he can picture coming in there. As he finishes, I lick my lips for him. I feel able to be dirtier with him than I would be with Jonathan, and it's empowering.

"Thank you," he says, then hangs up. I didn't even see his face or say a word, but fuck me, that was hot! My heart is still racing, my face and chest flushed as I lie in bed afterwards, going over it all in my head, wanting to firmly cement in my memory the feeling of being an object of sexual desire.

Chapter 7

Another Saturday comes around. We have nowhere to be and I'm anticipating a nice lie-in, with lazy morning sex. Maybe I'll even bring Jonathan breakfast in bed again. I snuggle into him, gently taking hold of his cock, but he bats me away.

"I need to get up. I want to put those shelves up in the kitchen today."

I don't care about the bloody shelves! I don't want to listen to drilling and hammering all day long, again. I just want his attention, and to spend some nice time together. I miss the fun, laidback Jonathan of the summer holidays, the one who actually seems to want to spend time with me. Even if he really does have to get up, I wish he could at least pretend he's disappointed about it and wishes he could stay.

But without so much as a kiss or cuddle, or a "maybe later," he's up and off to the bathroom to start with his day. I don't know why it surprises or disappoints me anymore, but it does. It leaves me feeling ugly and disgusting, rejected and unwanted. It makes me want to call Ellis again, or anyone really, who will make me feel good about myself, show me I'm worth something. I pull the covers up over my head with a sigh. I just want to hide away for a bit, feeling sorry for myself.

I pull myself together and have an idea. Whilst he's in the shower, I update my dating profile with a fake name, *Cassandra*, and send him a message from it.

He comes back from the bathroom, pottering around at a snail's pace as he gets dry and dressed, before finally looking at his phone.

His eyes light up and he opens the app. I worry this was a bad idea and he's about to be severely disappointed. But when he sees my Very Best Selfie—all sultry eyes, red, shiny lips, and big bombshell hair—there on his screen, he laughs.

"Are you going to message her?" I ask with a raised eyebrow, hoping he'll catch on quickly to my cunning plan to have a pretend first date, a dress rehearsal.

He starts to say something, but at my pointed facial expression, he stops himself. "Yeah, I guess so."

I smile at him before I grab my book and leave the room to lock myself away in the bathroom. I turn on the bath taps, pour in a generous glug of bubble bath, and slip slowly into a heavenly bath, the slightly too-hot water turning my skin pink immediately.

Once I'm settled in, I take a look at my phone and, surprise surprise, there's a message waiting for me!

Hi. He's not the most creative.

How are you?

Good, thanks.

You're really hot. I love tall guys.

Thanks. You too. Your hair is pretty.

Even these primary-school level compliments feel good, nicer than anything he's said to me in a long time.

What are you looking for on here? I ask him. Although I hate being asked that question, I want to see what he says.

I'm not sure. I've been with my girlfriend for seven years and we're happy, or I thought we were, but now she wants to open up our relationship. I'm not sure about it, but I want to give it a go for her.

Urgh. He's being exactly the kind of guy I'm already bored of meeting on here. But he's also being more honest and open with me than in our previous conversations, so I'll go with it. Maybe it'll help him see my perspective more easily too, help him understand me and why I want what I do. Even though I'm not entirely sure myself of exactly what I want or why. *That sounds hard. I'm in a similar situation, but it's me wanting to open up. I love my boyfriend so much, but I want a bit more fun and excitement in my life.*

Between leg shaving and losing myself reading *The Goldfinch*, we get into a nice conversation with each other, my fingers and toes becoming ever more wrinkled. It's easier than I expected to get into character. We're being ourselves, but versions from a parallel universe where we haven't met before now. It's fun, getting to know each other again.

So...what are you up to tonight? he asks me.

Is he asking me out? Even though we've been on a million dates together and he's right there downstairs, I feel a rush of excitement.

I leave the dating app for a moment to text him normally as my real self, his girlfriend, the one from this universe: *I'm going to go out tonight if you want the house to yourself.*

I'm hopeful the thumbs-up emoji I receive in return is confirmation that he's understood what I want to do.

On the app, Cassandra—the parallel universe version of me—tells him: *I've got no plans tonight.*

Excellent. My girlfriend is going out, so I have the house to myself if you'd like to come here for dinner?

Before I know it, we've got a date lined up. We avoid each other all day to build up the tension, like a real date. I stay mostly upstairs reading, whilst he heads to town. After his trip to the shops, I can hear him cleaning and cooking downstairs, mouth-watering smells of frying garlic and onions making their way up to me, the shelves forgotten for today at least. I take my time picking out what to wear, doing my hair and makeup. I'm genuinely excited.

Five minutes later than he's expecting me, I creep downstairs and out of the front door to ring the bell. He smiles as he opens the door, takes my jacket, and compliments my outfit—my favourite, most flattering dress. It's bright green, low-cut, cinched in at just the right place on my waist, and short but classy enough that I could wear it out for a nice meal. The kind of dress that makes you stand tall and proud and want to dance.

He's got changed too, into a shirt he's rolled up to the elbows, exposing his gorgeous forearms and their soft hairs and thin wrists, his left wrist adorned with the watch his parents gave him when he graduated university. Men's forearms are irresistible to me, their visibly toned strength next to the vulnerability of their inner wrists and elbows. The nobble where the little finger of the hand joins the arm. And their masterful, strong hands at the end of them. I love Jonathan's long, delicate fingers, the tiny hairs on his knuckles.

Jonathan pulls me from my distracted thoughts. "Would you like a drink? I have some white wine or beer."

"Perfect. Wine, please."

He leads me through to the dining table in the lounge, which is cleaner than I've ever seen it before. For once, the table isn't covered in school books, no pens and paper overflowing onto the floor and the arm of the sofa. The table is clear and laid beautifully for dinner, a big pillar candle lit in the centre. He's really made an effort to make this feel like a real date, and I can't help smiling in appreciation. "Dinner's almost ready if you want to take a seat," he says as he hands me a glass of wine and I sit down.

Over the course of the evening, we continue to stay in character, getting to know each other and asking about our respective partners and what they make of this whole thing. It's interesting to hear it in this way; we're saying things we haven't said to each other before, things we've said in different ways. It's somehow easier, like we're talking about characters from a film rather than each other.

"Do you think you'll ever want children?" I ask him.

"Definitely not any time soon. I love my life. I don't want anything to change. That's why all this is so hard. Sophie thinks that's boring, though. She wants a bit more excitement and adventure. We've been together for so long and since we were so young, she just wants to see what more there might be to life."

I smile back at him. It's so good to hear him explain it simply and confidently like this. Maybe he really is starting to understand me. "I can understand that. We're all pretty young to be all set up for life already. A bit of adventure keeps things interesting."

He's cooked his favourite: creamy mushroom gnocchi with garlic bread and rocket. It's delicious. I take my time over it, savouring the taste and the effort I know has gone into it, like I would on a real date, for fear of spilling it down myself or talking with my mouth full and putting him off forever. But I'm also eating more slowly because I'm enjoying our conversation, appreciating his company in a way I don't usually when we shovel our food down whilst plonked in front of the TV.

After we've eaten, we sit quietly, in the flickering flattering candlelight, gazing at each other. Seven years we've been together, but I can't remember the last time I looked at him like this. It's like I'm meeting him for the first time all over again.

Full of food and wine, we move to the sofa. To my absolute disbelief, Jonathan is happy to leave the washing up until the morning so we can be together now. Normally if we found ourselves in this position on a Saturday night, we'd just zone out in front of the TV and go off to bed. But tonight we don't turn the TV on, don't even stop to put any music on. We keep talking, back to being ourselves now, reminiscing about our past together, remembering our nervous first dates, meeting each other's parents for the first time—awkward teenagers playing grown-up.

When I initially had the idea for this date, I thought it would be sexy, that we'd have some amazing sex pretending to be strangers. But we don't have sex. We just have a really lovely evening getting to know each other all over again. In a way, it's much hotter than I expected.

Chapter 8

The sweet old couple have started coming into the café more regularly now. The man, who I now know as Frank, is such a gentleman, doing everything he can to look after his adoring wife, Ethel. Both of them have the brightest blue eyes that crinkle when they smile, which is often. They're always holding hands, publicly declaring their love for one another.

They usually come in towards the end of the day, when things are quiet and I'm just waiting to clean up and close, so I often find myself watching them or chatting to them with interest. Pride bursts out of Frank as he tells me about their two sons, even as he describes how they're too busy with their lives to visit very often, making me squirm with guilt as I realise I haven't spoken to my own parents in too long.

Their eldest son, Andy, lives about half an hour away and seems to take care of things like food shopping and driving them around. Their youngest son, Mike, is up in Scotland so he doesn't visit often, especially since his wife was diagnosed with MS. Between caring for her and their two children, he only manages to get down once or twice a year. But you can see Frank and Ethel light up when they talk about their grandchildren.

Although they're grown up now, about my age I think, they still love exploring their beloved garden just like when they were small.

It's almost closing time as Frank puts on his flat cap and helps Ethel into her coat so I can lock up. As they leave, they're intercepted by a whirlwind of curly red hair clashing irresistibly against a bright red coat—my best friend Amy. It's been a while since I've seen her; she broke up with her boyfriend a year ago and has been busy on a dating mission ever since, coming and going from my life depending on how infatuated she is at the time. We've been friends long enough that we can always pick up where we left off, no matter how long it's been. Although I do miss her sometimes, I don't resent her making the most of single life, and I know she'd be there for me if I really needed her.

"Soph! Long time, no see! How are you? Am I too late for a coffee?"

"I'm ready to lock up now. Come on, let's go to the pub."

Ten minutes later we're in the pub by the roaring fire, sharing a bottle of wine, catching up since the last time we saw each other. Our mouths water at the smell of a nearby table's vinegar-soaked chips and we order ourselves a bowl to share. She's loving life, still enjoying getting out there dating and not settling down. It sounds thrilling but also reminds me how much I do enjoy the stability of being with Jonathan, as boring as it may sometimes be.

Once she's finished updating me about the "hot-as-fuck crazy guy" she was with last night, I tell her about the kiss in Brighton, Jonathan's experience in Prague, how it's led to us opening up our relationship, and my recent kiss and the frustration that's followed. I tell her about downloading the dating app, our pretend date, and how it's brought us closer together. I tell her how, after each kiss with a stranger, our sex life has improved after so many years of predictability. At this, she balks. She's known Jonathan even longer than I have and doesn't want to think about him having sex with anyone, ever, thank you very much.

"Aren't you worried you'll end up splitting up?"

Am I? I take a moment to think about this. I don't think we will; I'm pretty confident in our relationship. I've already pushed Jonathan further than some couples could take and we've survived. If anything, we're stronger than ever now that I've been so honest with him and we've had to face up to some difficult truths. "No. People have affairs all the time and end up splitting up anyway. I think it's actually less likely this way. And if we do, we do. Any one of us could die tomorrow too. I'm not going to live my life based on fear of all the what-ifs."

It's only as I'm telling all of this to Amy that I realise what really kicked all this off for me. It was a couple of months before the Brighton kiss.

"When Jonathan proposed, I hadn't seen it coming. It scared me. I thought we were far too young and cool for something so grown-up and traditional. It made me realise I wanted something more from my life."

He'd proposed out of nowhere one day at lunch. He hadn't bought a ring or anything and the more we talked about it, the clearer it became he was about as interested in getting married as I was. He just thought we'd been together for too long and should do something to mark it. I think his mum might've had something to do with it. He didn't even seem disappointed or surprised when I said no. I'd never harboured ambitions of a big wedding or dressing up in an overpriced dress, only to tuck it away in a box never to be seen again. It just all seemed such a waste of money to me. I don't think I could've put it into words then, but I think the finality of it, promising never to be with anyone else ever again, made me uncomfortable. I knew it was a promise I wouldn't be able to keep.

After that lunch, neither of us mentioned it again and I hadn't really given it another thought before now.

"Soph, I need to go for an STI check, and you probably should too now just to be sure. Shall we go to the walk-in centre together tomorrow? It might be sort of fun to do it together?"

On the hard blue chairs in the quiet waiting room the next day, Amy and I have a little giggle at some of the more graphic pictures on the leaflets and posters. It feels awkward, like everyone knows why we're here. Last time we were in the family planning clinic together was when we were sixteen, I'd just lost my virginity with some awful guy at a house party who was rumoured to have already got one teenage girl pregnant, and Amy (who was a little older and more experienced in these matters) came with me to get the morning-after pill and a STI test. I feel just as awkward and nervous this time around, that awful feeling that someone will see me here and tell my mum.

My name is called before Amy's, and I follow the nurse down a long corridor into a nice and bright clinic room. Everything is very clean and there's a reassuringly sterile smell in the air. The nurse has an open, friendly appearance but there's a classic sternness to her too that tells me she takes no prisoners.

"What can I do for you today?"

I feel like an awkward teenager, squirming in my chair and not quite able to look her in the eye. Partly because we're talking about sex, but also because I feel a bit like I'm wasting her time. I haven't had sex with anyone but Jonathan for seven years, so I know nothing is going to come up on a test. "I'd like to get an STI test." And with that, I've set the ball rolling again. "I have a long-term partner and a contraceptive implant, but we're thinking of opening our relationship, so I want to be sure I'm safe first." I'm not quite sure how I expect her to react to this.

"That's really sensible. We'll just need to take some measurements, and then you'll do your own swab in the toilet. You'll get a text in a week or so to let you know if there are any concerns."

I let out a sigh of relief at how easy this all seems to be. Her calm reaction helps me feel normal and accepted and I'm relieved I told her. I walk out of that room lighter, even a little proud of myself for telling the truth.

I'm weighed and measured. She takes a small sample of blood, and then gives me a little kit to take into the toilet for my vaginal swab. I return to hand over my sample and am given a large paper bag full of condoms and sachets of lube in return.

And that's it! It was so much easier than I expected.

Chapter 9

With me laid out on the sofa munching on crisps in front of the TV, and Jonathan in the bedroom shouting at our new flat pack wardrobe, we don't exude the same happiness as Frank and Ethel from the café. We've been getting on better than ever since our date night, but I'm not sure I can picture us growing old together like that anymore; the thought fills me with a bored dread. If we're still together at that age, what will have happened in the meantime? Is this it now—we just carry on as we are, go to work, come home, eat, drink, watch TV, do some DIY, go to bed and do it all again tomorrow until one day our hair is white, but apart from that, nothing's really changed?

I think of my own parents, who've been together for almost thirty years and still appear to be happy about it. I wonder if they truly are, what secrets they might be hiding from each other or the world, but I'm not sure I'd ever want to ask. Ignorance is bliss.

A loud phone beep drags me from my existential thoughts.

A brief pause, and then he shows me his phone screen. "I've got a match!"

A match? I haven't gone on the app again since our date, and we haven't really talked about it, but this has to be a good sign. He seems excited; maybe he's more on board with all of this than I realised.

He smiles as he checks out the profile of this girl he's matched with: Sarah.

"Can I see?" I ask, and he willingly hands me his phone.

She looks nice. A bit older than me, which feels reassuring somehow. You don't ever hear of boyfriends running off with an older woman, do you? For the rest of the evening, he's distracted chatting with her, occasionally asking me to help him respond to a message, that huge smile staying on his face all night. It's like this Sarah has reignited a spark in him I haven't seen for a long time. That stings too; I want to do that for him. But I get it—it's how I've felt chatting to and kissing new people, and I'm glad he's getting that feeling for himself now. If nothing else, it might help him understand me better.

"Sarah wants to meet me next week. Is that okay?"

I don't know what's wrong with me. It's okay, of course it is. I can hardly say no. I'm pleased for him. I can see he's excited. But I am a bit jealous—I want this for myself. It's not fair. "Of course! That's really exciting!"

I haven't been on the app again since that first flurry of matches, which was all too overwhelming, and then again for our practice date, but I find myself on it again over the next couple of days. I know I should let Jonathan have his moment, his turn, but I can't resist.

I start flicking through profiles, swipe right on a few.

And that's when I see *him*.

Ben.

Soft brown curls highlighted by the sun (he's outdoorsy),

and pictured out in mountains (he's adventurous), tattoos and a nose ring (he's cool), just the right amount of stubble (he's sexy), dark eyes that seem to be staring deep into my soul (he's sensual), and the most gorgeous smile (he's fun). No description, but I don't need any. He looks like a rock star. I swipe right and pray he'll do the same.

This is torture. I've swiped right on several people so far but once I've swiped, I've moved on to the next one and generally forgotten who went before unless we match.

But I can't get Ben out of my head.

In the end I have to hide my phone away. It's not healthy checking it every five minutes like this. I watch *The IT Crowd* on TV to try and distract myself. Roy is on a bad date, a smudge of chocolate on his forehead mistaken for shit. What if I match with this guy and do something that embarrassing on our date? Maybe I'm not cut out for this after all. Maybe it's more trouble than it's worth. My palms feel sweaty and uncomfortable, my whole body twitchy, and I can't sit still.

Finally, I give in and allow myself to check my phone. He's matched with me! Seven minutes ago, he sent me a message: *Hi, how are you?*

My heart is racing. I can't believe this is happening. I hide my phone again in an effort to not reply too soon and come on too strong, and to pull myself together a bit.

After a full thirty-two minutes, I can wait no longer and send him a reply. Before I know it, the conversation is flowing.

So, what are you looking for here? he asks me.

I take my time over my response. I want to be honest with him, but not scare him off. *Well, I have a boyfriend, but I want some extra fun to spice things up a bit. But I want more than hook-ups. I want it to be at least friends with benefits, getting together*

44

about once a month, having nice dates as well as sex.

That sounds good to me! Would you like go out for a drink on Saturday?

I like how forward he is—it's flattering.

"I've matched with someone too," I tell Jonathan. "He's asking if I want to meet for a drink on Saturday. Is that okay with you?"

I see the cogs turning in Jonathan's head, dealing with the same emotions I had when he told me about Sarah. But with an extra element I haven't given enough consideration to:

"Can't you just let me meet Sarah first?"

He's right. It's definitely his turn. I'm stealing his thunder. It's not a competition; I want to feel like it's fair for us both. We both do. Begrudgingly, I give in. "Okay. I'll tell him I can't make it. He'll probably just think I'm playing it cool on purpose!"

As willingly as I delay the date, I can't help my mind going down a rabbit hole, convinced Ben will match with someone else in the meantime because I've made him wait. What if that someone else turns out to be Sarah? They're both local, both on the same app—it would make sense. Maybe they should just be together anyway, leave us out of it. That would be so much easier all round. Maybe all four of us should go on a double date. My head is spinning with the possibilities.

"I told Sarah I'd organise our date. She's not lived here long, so I said I'd take her somewhere new, somewhere she might not find otherwise. I thought it seemed romantic to take charge like that, but now I don't know what to organise. Can you help me?"

I can't help but smile as I notice how nervous he is, his eyes wide and hopeful like a puppy pleading for one more throw of

45

its ball. He wants my help, but this is so out of the ordinary that I think he's worried I'll say no. He's wrong, though. This is exactly the kind of opportunity I've been looking forward to. I'm pleased he's letting me get involved without me having to feel like I'm being nosy. "What sort of thing are you thinking?"

"I don't know! What do you think?"

"What about crazy golf, or a roller disco, or the cinema, or bowling, or those High Ropes in the forest?" I'm getting excited myself here! Although, if he does take her on a date like that, I will be jealous—he never wants to do anything like that with me.

"I think that sounds too much for a first date. I want to keep it simple. So we can escape easily enough if we don't hit it off. Just a drink or something is probably enough. Isn't it?"

"Okay, so what's she like?"

"She seems pretty wholesome. I want to take her somewhere nice, but nothing fancy. It might feel too full on. A country pub or something maybe. Might be good to go somewhere new to me as well; then I won't be worried about seeing someone who knows me."

I get searching online, searching for ideas, and find an old country pub and a short circular walk from it. We agree to go and scout it out together at the weekend. This could work out well—we get a nice date together, he gets a date with her, and then hopefully he'll be all excited about it afterwards and that'll make him horny and really into me the way he was after the girl in Prague.

Chapter 10

"There it is! It's perfect!"

A big old white pub, complete with thatched roof and roses around the doorway, comes into view and it's just right: cosy and homely looking. Framed by an almost too-perfect blue sky adorned with white fluffy clouds. I feel like I'm inside a postcard. We drive a little further and find somewhere to park and set off on our walk.

I've got all the instructions up on my phone and they lead us down the hill, away from the little village. Suddenly we find ourselves walking on the main road—seemingly the correct route, according to the instructions, but this road is far busier than I expected from the description. It's more stressful and polluted than the nice nature walk we were hoping for.

Soon we find a gap in the hedge and the public footpath that leads us across fields and along the path of a meandering river, orange leaves shining brightly on the trees and under our feet. This is more like it! The sounds of the busy road disappear quickly, and it feels like we're in the middle of nowhere. It's peaceful. A beautiful old humpback bridge takes us across the river, and we follow the path up the hill into the woods. Checking against the map, I realise we've gone off course, so we head back on ourselves and try to find the right path.

The right path is there. We missed it the first time because of the electric fence and *No Entry* sign that crosses it.

"Shall we go back the way we came, or try up the hill again?"

Determined, we head back up the hill in search of an alternative route. A pretty path leads us through the woods until we come out onto a field full of huge cows. I've been vegetarian since I was eleven, but the cows don't know that. Jonathan has been vegetarian too since the horsemeat scandal earlier this year (although it's beyond me why people are so horrified at the thought of eating a horse when they'll quite happily tuck into a cow or chicken... but if it's making more people go vegetarian, then I'm not complaining). And I'm not sure how they'd feel about us drinking their milk anyway. Don't walkers get killed by cows all the time?

Before I have too much time to worry about it, Jonathan is over the stile and confidently crossing the field, and I have no choice but to follow. I'm certainly not planning on shouting and drawing attention to myself.

As I climb over the stile and try to catch up with Jonathan, it starts to rain, a real downpour that's come out of nowhere, soaking through my hoodie almost instantly. It's a huge relief to come out of the field, turn a corner, and realise we're on the outskirts of the village. "There it is! I can see the pub!"

He takes my hand and we run, laughing, to the pub. We're both gasping for a pint, so when we walk up to the door, we push straight into it, completely missing the *Closed for Refurbishment* sign stuck to it.

"I think you're going to have to come up with another idea, but at least you've got a good story for your date."

We drive home in our wet clothes, laughing with each other

about our disastrous date attempt and whether we should take it as a sign that this is all a terrible idea. Arriving home, we strip off immediately, throwing our wet clothes straight into the washing machine.

"Follow me," I say, grabbing his hand and pulling him up the stairs.

We have lovely, messy period sex, falling asleep on bloody sheets afterwards, too tired to change them.

After our disastrous recce, Jonathan came up with a less risky location for his date with Sarah, a cosy little café on the outskirts of town. He was adorable getting ready; I've never seen him so nervous. He even had a clean shave and changed his outfit three times as he couldn't quite decide what to wear.

As happy as I am—excited, even—for him to be there and for it to go well, I'm anxious for him to get home and tell me all about it. I can't relax. I want to know what's going on. I'm desperate for it to go well, for him to understand why I want this and to even things out between us. Selfishly, I know the better it goes, the more okay he'll be about me seeing Ben. But I'm also scared that if it doesn't go well, he won't let me meet Ben at all.

Dreamy Ben, who texts me every evening to ask about my day. Dreamy Ben, who sends me pictures of himself fresh from the shower, beads of water resting on his beautiful skin, stretched over a perfectly toned body and decorated with colourful tattoos. Dreamy Ben, who somehow appears to find me as attractive as I find him.

Finally, Jonathan comes home, where he finds me in the bath, halfway through a bottle of red wine, unable to concentrate on my book. I was wishing he would've said when he expected to be back so I could've relaxed and enjoyed the time to myself a bit more. It's only been a few hours, but I was restless waiting for him.

"Is there room for me in there?" he asks, his eyebrow raised, starting to take off his clothes. He slides into the other end of the bath, our bodies comfortably finding their familiar spots intertwined with each other, my feet resting on his shoulders, my big toes touching his ears, his feet squished into the sides of the bath around my bum.

"How was it?"

"It was fun. She was lovely. Sweet." The goofy grin on his face suggests she was better than lovely and sweet. God, he looks sexy right now; it's like she's given him a confidence boost that's shining out of his every pore. "I was telling her all about you, and she said you sounded amazing and she'd like to meet you. That feels like a step too far for me, though. I think it's better that these things are all kept separate."

Knowing he must've been saying good things about me fills me with happiness, although I'm disappointed I won't get to meet her.

"When I was coming back home, I was driving toward a rainbow the whole way. It was so beautiful," he says dreamily.

I let out a little laugh. Who is this person talking about rainbows? And when is he going to get to the good stuff? "And... ?"

"And?"

"Did anything happen?"

"We kissed goodbye. But I don't think I fancy her."

I'm not sure I believe that, however certain he seems of it. He's so...energised. Surely, he can only have got that buzz from some kind of desire for her? Or maybe knowing she liked him enough to kiss him is enough of a boost for him?

As the water gradually gets colder around us, he tells me more about the date: how nervous he was, what they talked about, how easy it felt talking to her, what the kiss was like. (He says she leaned in for the kiss first, but he says that about our first kiss, and I know it was the other way round—I was never confident enough to make the first move back then.)

I want to know what all of this means for me and my date, but I know I need to hold my tongue for now.

Chapter 11

By the morning, I can hold my tongue no more, and I broach the subject of meeting Ben. Jonathan can't really say no now he's had a date of his own, so it's an easy enough conversation, but I'm worried we'll end up in a tit-for-tat situation, which I'm sure can't be a good idea.

Ben seems so sweet, and I am so completely and utterly physically attracted to him, so I make no hesitation when he suggests meeting at his. I like knowing we can't get caught out in public by someone I know. The rules seem different; there's no pretence that I'm trying to find my future husband, so I don't feel the need to play games. It feels safe too. He knows that Jonathan is waiting for me to come home and that he knows where I am.

Half of me is worried he'll get too attached to me and want more from me than I can give. Even thinking that might be possible gives me a confidence boost, though. The other half of me is worried we'll start something good and then he'll meet someone else who's single and he'll have to stop seeing me even if things are good with us. But perhaps I'm getting ahead of myself.

In the days leading up to the date, I discover an energy that wasn't there before. I eat salads for lunch and don't stuff my face with chocolate and crisps in the evenings.

On the morning itself, I wake up early and dig out my old sports bra and trainers to go for a run. With one foot in front of the other, I get into a hot and sweaty mess in no time, running around the park. I've not been out of the house this early in a long time; it's so peaceful with fewer cars on the roads, the birds singing their morning song. I run past one bush full of birds so loud it's almost unpleasant, and as I do, they erupt out of the bush and into the sky like lava from a volcano. There aren't many people out in the park just yet, but those I see—other runners, dog walkers—all look cheerful, full of hope and optimism for the day ahead.

As I find a more comfortable rhythm, I start to lose myself in thoughts of tonight's date. I put together various possible outfits in my head, unsure what's expected when I'm going straight to his. A nice dress I'd wear out for a meal or night out seems too much, but would jeans or leggings seem too casual? I keep on running, mentally filing through my wardrobe, but nothing seems to quite fit the bill. I don't want to seem like I'm trying too hard, but I don't want it to look like I don't care, either.

My thoughts turn to Jonathan and how he's going to be whilst I'm out and when I get back. Now he's had a date himself; I hope he can remember how good it felt but that it didn't stop him from wanting to come home. But I know I was getting impatient whilst he was out, wanting him back, and I genuinely wanted him to be meeting Sarah! We've agreed I'll come home by eleven p.m. as a way of building trust (because nothing bad ever happens before eleven, right?), but is there anything else I could do that I've not thought of? I'm so desperate for this to go well; in fact, I'm more anxious for Jonathan to have a good evening than I am for my date to be a success.

Legs aching and heart racing, I stop to catch my breath. It's only when I check my phone that I realise I've run 5k! That's a respectable distance—people collect sponsorship for Race for Life and that's 5k! I didn't even know I could run that far. Suddenly my worries seem smaller. With all these endorphins pumping through my body, I feel I can do anything. I'm ready to conquer the world.

I've had health kicks like this in the past, but as soon as I realise Jonathan doesn't really notice or care, I wonder what it's all for and give up. He would say of course that he likes me just the way I am, that his love goes deeper than how I look. I know I'm lucky to have him, but I wish sometimes he'd be overcome with lust and the need to ravage me.

Later that afternoon, it's finally time to start getting ready, a process I thoroughly enjoy. I have a long, hot bath, taking my time to shave my legs and armpits thoroughly, enjoying the strawberry bubbles. After my bath, skin still pink, I sit on my bed wrapped in a big fluffy towel, staring into my wardrobe, hoping inspiration will hit me. I slather myself in fruity body lotion and lie on the bed, allowing it to absorb fully.

I get out of bed, drop my towel, and assess my naked body in the mirror as I brush my hair. Straight on, I think I look pretty good, my thin waist tapering out into wider hips. But from the side, I can hardly face the mirror, my stomach protruding almost triangularly from the rest of my body. I must remember to breathe in tonight.

I'm feeling more nervous now. Rummaging through my clothes, I decide that dressing more casually might help counteract my nerves, giving me the appearance of being carefree and chilled about this whole thing. Leggings and a (nice) t-shirt it is.

But what about underwear? My usual underwear definitely won't do. Whether or not he gets to see it, I want to know what's under my clothes looks good. I pull out a black lacy bralette, deciding this will complete the chilled-out vibe I'm going for. And I decide against pants altogether; my bum will be smoother in my leggings without any, and it might be hot if he can tell I'm not wearing them.

Next up is makeup. I layer on moisturiser and then foundation. My cheeks are still unacceptably red, so I add concealer to try to even them out a bit before brushing on blusher to make them rosy red again. Finally, I brush dark mascara through my lashes and finish off with tinted lip balm.

I take a deep breath and go to Jonathan, who's marking schoolwork in the lounge. "I'm ready to go now. How are you doing?"

"I'm okay. Is that what you're wearing?"

"Don't start," I warn him, not entirely sure if he's joking or not.

"You look lovely."

"So you've got Ben's address. I'll be home by eleven and I'll check in with you once I've met him, so you know I'm safe."

"Okay. Good luck," he says with a smile I think is genuine.

On my way to Ben's, I stop in the local Superdrug for condoms, something I've never had to buy myself—in our early days, Jonathan always bought them and then I went on the pill and then the implant, my second one still buried safely in my arm. To my horror, they only have enormous boxes of them. It seems a little presumptuous, turning up with a giant box of condoms, so I take out a couple and put them in my pocket, stuffing the rest of the box deep into my bag and hoping it stays hidden away. It's only as I'm doing this that I remember the nice discreet package I was given at the walk-in centre, which is still unopened in our bathroom cupboard.

With a deep breath, I'm on my way now.

Am I really going to do this?

Chapter 12

As I walk up the crunchy gravel path leading to Ben's front door, I don't dare take even the briefest of moments to think about what I'm doing, for fear I'll change my mind. Before I can ring the doorbell and take a moment to compose myself, the door is open.

Fuck. He's even hotter than in his pictures, hotter than in my wildest imagination. I catch my mouth as it drops open with a sigh of desire, my eyes wide, taking him all in. I try my best to turn it into a polite, friendly smile rather than the look of a dog in heat.

He smiles at me as he opens the door wider and points me towards his lounge, where I make myself comfortable on the enormous squidgy sofa. You can tell this is the house of a man who lives alone. It's all grey and purposeful, a giant TV mounted on the wall but not a picture or anything purely decorative in sight, not even a mirror. Everything seems very clean, the faint smell of polish in the air, and I'm not sure if it's because he's cleaned for me or he's just a bit anal.

As he comes into the room, our eyes lock. It's as if a magnet is pulling me up off the sofa towards him, my lips to his, and I taste his minty breath as we kiss like a pair of horny teenagers.

My legs are jelly.

His kiss is soft and tender but somehow rough and needy at the same time, his tongue warm as it pushes into my mouth. My nervousness has disappeared now, replaced with lust and desire that makes my heart beat even faster. I feel like the sexiest woman in the world. I reach up to his face, his neck, his earlobes between my fingers. His hands feel warm and firm on my waist.

Inquisitively he plays with the hem of my top, gazing deep into my eyes as he pushes it up a little. Not wanting to waste any time, I pull my top up over my head, exposing the black lace beneath.

This is the first time I've undressed in front of someone other than Jonathan since I was a teenager, and the first time I've ever been in this situation sober with a new person. Ben has a grin on his face and a sparkle in his eyes that banishes whatever body confidence issues I might've had. I feel on top of the world, a total goddess.

Still kissing me, he expertly removes my bra before burying his face in my chest, my nipples hardening for him as I let out a moan. He licks his way slowly down my body as he moves to the floor. His tongue is so soft, setting my skin alight with pleasure. Kneeling at my feet, he separates my legs and dives face-first into me. His tongue hungrily flicks over my clit, those beautiful eyes focused on mine the whole time. I want to keep staring into his beautiful eyes. Every time I do it feels even more intense, but very intimate too, a little too much. I can't stop myself from looking away, closing my eyes.

His fingers slip inside me and find just the right spot, stroking me in time with his tongue. It's like he can read my mind; he knows what I want and is doing it before I've even thought of it. I throw my head back and cry out in pleasure but keep returning to those gorgeous eyes. This is an image I'm going to be thinking of a lot in future and I want to memorise every single pixel, sear it into my mind forever.

His pace quickens and, with my eyes finally properly on his, I melt. I've never come whilst standing before—my legs are weak, my breath fast and shallow. He gently but firmly pushes me down to the sofa as he reaches to a side table, where he has a condom at the ready (I could've saved myself the trip!) and puts it on. This isn't like the awkward condom moments of my teenage sexual encounters; he knows exactly what he's doing and makes no complaints about using one. I'm glad of the recovery time—I've only just caught my breath as he rises up and plunges his cock deep inside me and fucks me hard and fast, his determined eyes never leaving mine. I can't believe this is really happening, I want to pinch myself. I want to take a picture, even a video, so I can remember it forever.

Unexpectedly he pulls out, but to my surprise and delight, it's so he can go down on me again. His eyes never leave mine as he kisses and sucks and licks away. My moans get louder and more intense. I have no control over the sounds that are leaving me. I can feel blood vessels in my face bursting with the intensity of it. I'm breathless with pleasure and desire; I don't want this to end ever.

My hands are in his hair, which feels soft and clean. As his tongue licks me harder, I let out a whimper and pull away a little. It's almost too much for me to take, but instead of giving me a break, he hooks his arms around my legs, pulling me even closer into him. He builds momentum and gets faster and faster until suddenly...*yes!* The strongest, deepest orgasm of my life, a waterfall of pure pleasure, flows out of me. An embarrassing amount of juices squirt all over his face and hand, his sofa and his jeans. I'm not entirely sure if that was hot or disgusting, but he has an accomplished look on his face and doesn't appear to make any attempt to wipe it away, so I'm going to go with hot, although we do share an awkward grin.

He moves his arms around my body and slowly pulls me back up to standing. His face still glistening with my juices, he kisses me before turning me around to lean my hands on the back of the sofa. He stands behind me and starts to fuck me. His hand moves to my belly and I'm suddenly self-conscious, wanting to curl around it and hide away but knowing that will only make it feel bigger to him. I straighten my back in an attempt to flatten my belly, but again I needn't have worried—he seems to love holding onto me.

He picks me up with him in those beautiful, strong arms and moves me to the floor, as though I'm as light as a little rag doll. He starts fucking me doggy style, his cock so big it almost hurts. As I loudly cry out in pleasure, he clamps his hand around my mouth, and I suck hard on his fingers.

I feel the change in tone as he gets closer to his climax; he's more focused on himself now. Keeping a perfect rhythm until the last moment before he pulls out and removes the condom to allow his warm come to cover my ass. We're both breathing hard, my head spinning with pleasure whilst I attempt to remember every single moment of the sex.

He disappears to get rid of the condom and, still on all fours, I take the opportunity to quickly reach for my phone and text Jonathan to confirm I'm safe and most definitely having a great time.

Ben comes back, wiping sweat from his forehead with a towel (this fit guy just fucked me so hard that he's drenched in sweat!)

which he then uses to wipe his come off me. There's something so tender about him caring for me like that after fucking me so hard.

We lie naked on the floor together as we recover and return to reality. He smells so good, a musty aftershave smell beneath the sweet, fresh sweat.

"Hi," he says, and only then do I realise we haven't even spoken so far, not a single word. I wonder if I should feel used at that thought, but I don't. I feel fucking irresistible, sexy and desired in a way I never have before.

"Hi," I reply, smiling.

I kiss him and run my hands over his perfectly toned muscles. I've never been with someone with such a beautiful body. I'd have been content just looking at him! He pulls a blanket over us, and we lie there, sleepily kissing and talking for an hour or so.

He tells me about his ex-girlfriend. They split up a year ago, but he still loves her, I can tell. I like that he's able to talk about her with me. It feels like he trusts me. "My friends keep telling me I should get out there, start dating, but I'm just not ready yet."

What is this then? I want to ask, but don't.

It's getting late, so I put my clothes on and get ready to leave. At the door he gives me another phenomenal kiss, leaving me weak at the knees.

"You're so fucking hot," I say without thinking, my face instantly hot.

"You are," he replies, and I think I might drown in happiness.

Chapter 13

Heading home, I alternate between making involuntary sex noises and little disbelieving giggles to myself about what just happened. I realise he didn't ask me a single question about myself, but that's okay. I liked listening to him, and I hope talking to me might even have helped him a bit.

Back home, I bounce into the house like an excited puppy.

"Looks like you had a good time. How was it?" Jonathan seems curious but perhaps a little apprehensive too, like he doesn't know what to expect or how he's going to react.

I take a breath. "How much do you want to know?"

"I'm not sure."

"Shall I just give you the headlines then?"

"Okay."

"We had sex, with a condom. And I squirted so much it was actually embarrassing; it went all over him!"

I watch Jonathan wince and know I've gone too far. I should've calmed down a bit, maybe called Amy or Lucy to tell them about it first. I guess I needed someone to confirm for me whether it was hot or embarrassing, normal or strange. But Jonathan isn't the person to do that. And given that he's been with me for as long as I've been with him, I'm not sure he even knows anyway.

We go straight to bed. He doesn't touch me or kiss me or say a word, but neither does he suggest that we should sleep separately. I feel bad; I'm having to physically hold myself back from reaching out to touch and comfort him, anticipating him rejecting me, pushing me away. I remind myself that I haven't done anything wrong. I kept within the rules we agreed to. Surely, it's better that I had a great time and still came home to him than getting swept up in wanting to be with Ben? Or even worse, put Jonathan through all this heartache and have a crappy date so neither of us is happy anyway? If he was hoping I'd have an awful time and decide none of this is worth it, then he's definitely disappointed, but I can't believe he would've hoped for that. I just want him to be happy for me that I had a good time. Is that really so much to ask?

I understand that he finds this difficult—of course he does; he's spent his whole life believing that having sex with someone who isn't your partner is wrong. It's going to take time and effort to change that mindset. I guess part of me hoped that once it actually happened, he'd realise it wasn't as bad as he thought, that he might even be turned on, that I could tell him about it and we could have amazing sex like we used to.

I was feeling like such a goddess, and I'm sure it would've been amazing if only he'd been open to it. I'm left feeling confused, half of me still buzzing from what happened with Ben, and the other disappointed that Jonathan has reacted more positively. I'm kicking myself for saying too much and ruining what should have been a lovely reconnection time.

63

Chapter 14

The weeks that follow are hard. I can see Jonathan is fighting an internal battle with himself. He doesn't want to be angry with me. I followed the rules we'd set together: checked in, used a condom, came home by eleven as promised. But it's clear he doesn't think sex is something that should happen on a first date, that he didn't even consider it might happen. I feel a bit angry with him for being so naïve, but pointing this out wouldn't help matters. He's disgusted with me—he'd never do something like this, so what kind of person must Ben be to do it? It's hard not to feel ashamed of myself, even though I don't think I did anything wrong.

"It's my body, so it should be up to me if I want to have sex with someone or not, shouldn't it? I just want my freedom and control over the decisions I make with my own body."

Jonathan looks a little downtrodden at this and takes a minute to respond, a long, painful minute for me, but I'm glad he seems to be taking it on board, thinking it through properly. "I know that. I get it in theory. It makes sense, I know. But when it comes down to it, it's so hard. I just wish we could go back to normal, that I'd never said I was okay with any of this or that you could feel like you've had your fill, but I know it's too late now."

"What are you scared of? You know I love you, and I want to be with you, and I love having sex with you. This isn't about you."

"I know. I guess it doesn't feel fair. This new person gets all the good bits, the fun and sex, whilst I'm here doing all the boring stuff and picking up the pieces if things don't work out for you."

"But you don't want to have sex as much as I do—that's the whole point! And that boring stuff is what ties us together and makes us closer, sets our relationship apart from any others. I really thought you were going to say you were worried we'd split up."

He takes a moment to think about this, as if this fear never even occurred to him. "I'm not scared you'll leave me. I do understand that. If anything, I'm scared I'll be so disgusted by you having sex with someone else that I'll have to leave you, that I'll begin to think of you as a slut and lose respect for you. The thought of someone else putting his dick in you makes me feel sick." He looks surprised at himself here, and I can't help wondering if it's the first time he's put this into words, even to himself. I don't want him to feel disgusted by me, but at least he's being more open and honest now.

"But if it's a girl, that's okay, is it?"

"Yeah, I think so. It wouldn't bother me as much. But you're not into that, anyway, are you?"

"I don't think I am, but it shouldn't make any difference. I don't think being a slut is a bad or shameful thing, no matter who I sleep with. I'm not ashamed that I want to have sex with more people than just you. Quite the opposite, in fact—I'm proud of myself for being honest about it and trying to do it right."

"I'm proud of you, too. I know it's not been easy for you and I've not helped with that, either. I just always thought that sex should be a sacred thing, something we only share with each other. It's hard to get past that. And I'm scared of where all this might lead. It started off with random kisses in clubs, now it's dates and sex. What comes next? Moving in together, having children with someone else? If I let you have too much now, I'm worried I'm opening the floodgates and it'll become out of control."

I feel like he's broken down a barrier at last, let me in, explained what's making it so hard for him. I don't plan to move in with anyone else or have babies with anyone, but I can see his point. The unknown scares him as much as it excites me. I don't know how to respond. I pull him in close to me. "I'm sorry this is so hard. Thank you for trying. We'll find our way in the end."

Chapter 15

December in the café is always fun. Everyone seems so cheerful and festive, coming in wearing their Christmas hats and novelty earrings, carrying bursting bags of Christmas shopping. We've got a big tree covered in twinkly fairy lights, which makes up for the fact we don't really bother with Christmas at home since we have so few visitors. Mince pies, stollen (my favourite), and Christmas cake keep the customers pouring in to warm up after their shopping trips.

I've started helping out a bit more in the kitchen now, suggesting new things for the menu and getting stuck into decorating gingerbread snowmen, Christmas trees, and reindeer. Lucy brings her girls in one day, buzzing from seeing Father Christmas in the shopping centre, and I let them decorate their own biscuits. They have lots of fun doing it, getting covered in icing and decorations in the process.

Frank and Ethel are tucking into a shared slice of Christmas cake and watching the girls with a smile. Ethel is as entranced by all the Christmas decorations as the girls, so I ask if she'd like to decorate her own biscuit too. Before I know it, she's sat with the girls and the three of them are having a wonderful time chatting away as they decorate their biscuits. Frank sits quietly on his own, watching Ethel with a smile, but he has a sadness about him too.

"Are you free tonight?" I ask Lucy. "I'm meeting a friend for a few festive drinks if you'd like to join us." Even as the words are coming out of me, I'm regretting them, hoping she'll say she's busy. What will Lucy and Amy make of each other? They're so different. Three's a crowd—everyone knows that.

"Oh, yes please, I'd love to. It's been a long week!"

My fears about Lucy and Amy getting on disappear within minutes of introducing them, as they immediately get lost in comfortable conversation, countless sugary fruity cocktails helping them along. Unfortunately though, their best chat seems to involve taking the piss out of me, with Amy telling Lucy various embarrassing stories from our schooldays. As Amy begins the story about me tripping over as I entered the stage in our Year Eleven school production of *Bugsy Malone*, ending up sprawled across the stage in front of the whole school, I decide enough is enough and I need to take control.

"So, I met a guy."

This does the trick; I have their attention now.

I tell them all about meeting Ben and the amazing sex we had, and I'm sure I see Amy's ears prick up. I realise they're both single and attractive and there's nothing stopping her from potentially meeting him and fucking him too, or even becoming his girlfriend. I feel territorial at this thought, even though in theory I shouldn't have a problem with it. It makes me want to see him again, to get some reassurance from him, but we've decided to leave it until after Christmas.

As Lucy gets progressively more drunk, she opens up more about her own sex life, or lack of it, the guilt she has for not wanting it, feeling like she's failing as a wife. Judging by how she's all ears when I talk about Ben, I'm not sure I'm convinced she's as uninterested in sex as she says.

We go out dancing and have a brilliant night singing along to cheesy Christmas hits, the same type of music I was rolling my eyes at last time I went out with Lucy making me smile this time, my cheeks aching from grinning so much. Occasionally a guy tries to break into our happy little triangle. It's the most empowering feeling in the world, knowing if I really fancied someone, I could kiss them tonight, that it's my own personal choice and not the automatic *I've got a boyfriend* it has been for so long. Tonight, though, I'm having far too much fun with my friends, and I'm too smitten with both Ben and Jonathan to even consider whether any of these other guys are hot or not.

We fall out of the club at the end of the night and go our separate ways. I love walking home at night, the fresh air sobering me up a bit and reducing my hangover the following day. I love hearing the pubs closing up for the night, hordes of people gathering around the kebab shops, drawn in by the smell of food. But as I get farther from the busy town and closer to home, the usual nervousness kicks in—being a girl walking alone at night never feels entirely safe, even somewhere I know so well. I keep my phone in my hand, poised to make a call or use it as a torch if I need to.

I see a man walking with a slow stumble ahead of me and know I'll have to pass him. I pull out my phone and pretend to be chatting to a friend so he won't bother me, won't try to talk to me or touch me, and so he knows I can call for help immediately if he does try anything.

I pass him without incident, a sense of relief flooding through me as I move farther away from him.

As soon as I get home, bread cooking away in the toaster and lashings of butter at the ready, I text Lucy and Amy: *Home now. Had a great night. So glad you two got on so well xx*

Lucy replies first: *I'm home too. Room spinning!*

Followed by Amy: *Night night xx*

Chapter 16

Jonathan and I are driving up to visit my parents on Christmas Eve when Jonathan's face suddenly drops and he turns the radio off.

"What's going on?" I ask, a clunking sound answering my question.

"Something's not right. The steering's gone funny—it keeps pulling over to one side. I think we might have a flat tyre or something. I'm going to pull over and have a look."

We pull over and as we get out of the car, the smell of burning is overpowering. The back tyre is destroyed.

"Fuck! What should we do? Should I call the AA?" I ask.

"It'll be okay. I can sort it," he says with a little laugh at my panic.

I hover around in the cold at the side of the road, trying to be helpful whilst Jonathan calmly changes the tyre, lying on the icy ground as he jacks the car up. "At least it's not raining!" I joke cheerily.

He glares back at me, and I realise he might not be quite as calm and collected as he appears.

I'm distracted by watching Jonathan with his hands, being so...manly, black grease and oil staining his fingers. I wonder what I would've done if I were by myself in this situation and know I would've had to call a breakdown service. I'm disappointed in myself. I want to be more self-sufficient than this, less reliant on a man or anyone else. I make myself a new year's resolution to learn to change a tyre so I could get through this situation even by myself without panicking.

We arrive at my parents' council estate an hour later than we were supposed to, the curtains in the lounge twitching as we drive toward the house and the door is wide open with Mum in it, hands on her hips and shaking her head before we've even got out of the car. Apparently, we've ruined all of my mum's dinner plans, despite us giving her plenty of warning that we were running late. It turns out these elaborate dinner plans are just a cold buffet anyway, so I'm not entirely sure what the fuss is about.

I'm distracted throughout dinner by the sight of a smudge of oil on Jonathan's neck, reminding me of how sexy I found him earlier. I haven't found him this alluring since he came back from Prague and told me about kissing that girl. We've barely had sex since Ben and I'm frustrated but biding my time, waiting for Jonathan to show me he's okay by making the first move.

There's an unwritten rule that we don't have sex at my parents' house. It's like they still think we're seventeen, and in response I find myself regressing back to being a lazy, stroppy teenager whenever I visit. I'm already excited to get home and ravish Jonathan.

Christmas morning comes, and Mum has done a huge break-fast, far too much food for just the four of us. We stuff our faces with hot croissants and fresh fruit, followed by a fry up and then more tea and toast than anyone could ever need. The sound of a Buck's Fizz bottle popping open gives the morning an appropriately celebratory feel.

I watch my parents over breakfast, wondering if they're happy, how they've stayed together so long, and what secrets might be lurking in their pasts. Dad used to work away a lot on whatever building site would take him when his bad back would allow, and Mum was always juggling two or three jobs trying to make ends meet. They were barely home, and both must've had opportunities to see other people. When they were home, they fought a lot. Dad felt guilty for not being able to work and provide for us, and Mum was always exhausted from trying to do everything for everyone. I never saw her sit down. Even when everything was done, she'd find something else to do, as if she had to keep busy because if she stopped for breath, everything would fall apart.

It was a stressful house to live in. We were warned against answering the door for fear of bailiffs coming to collect various debts. If we answered the door and let them in, it would be game over. Even now, when someone comes to my house unexpectedly, the sound of the doorbell sends me into a little panic.

Have they stayed together because they really wanted to, or for me and Tom? Or did it just never occur to them that splitting up was an option or something they could afford to do?

I wonder if they talk about me the way Frank and Ethel talk about their sons, but I know they don't. I haven't done anything for them to be proud of. I haven't given them any grandchildren to boast about, not had a big wedding for them to get stuck into, and I'm still just working in a café. And none of

73

this is likely to change anytime soon—mainly because I don't want it to. I'm happy with things as they are.

My brother Tom, on the other hand, can do no wrong. But that's easy from across the Atlantic, where he lives in his fancy New York apartment with his boyfriend and his high-flying job that keeps him so busy he can never come home, or even invite us to visit. I've still got no idea how he managed to get out there. One minute he was toiling away doing something with a magazine in London (his Media Studies degree obviously got him somewhere, whatever Dad might've made of it), and the next he'd come out as gay and was off to New York on some kind of transfer.

I wonder how much it would add to their disappointment if I told them that not only do we not intend to give them grandchildren or a wedding, but that we're opening up our relationship and having sex with other people.

All these thoughts of failure and letting my parents down have put me into a bad mood which no-one can understand. The reversion to teenager is complete. I avoid having to put on a cheery face by hiding in the kitchen doing the washing up, plunging my hands into the warm, soapy water and enjoying the familiar view of their long, thin garden, a large patch of dirt at the end which should be a vegetable patch, if only they could be bothered to do anything with it. The time on my own sorts me out a bit. I make another round of tea and return with a smile.

"Come on then. Shall we open some presents?"

Our presents are generally small and unimaginative: socks, whisky, bubble bath, a candle, but there's still something exciting about opening them. Jonathan and I don't really bother with presents but do exchange one small gift each.

I laugh as I open mine and realise it's the same thing I've bought him: Muse's *Black Holes and Revelations* on vinyl, the soundtrack to our first summer together as a couple.

Laughing, I hand him his present to open and see him smile as the penny drops.

I don't think I've ever loved him so much as in this moment, as our brains obviously work more similarly than we give them credit for. I go to give him a thank you kiss but it turns into a bit more of a snog, which is brought quickly to an end by my dad coughing pointedly.

In bed later after a thankfully short game of Charades, full of nut roast (much to Dad's dismay) and Christmas pudding, Jonathan and I forget all about the not-having-sex-in-my-parents'-house thing and have comfortable, slow and cuddly sex as he sings Muse in my ear.

Ben and I exchange Christmas bedtime wishes and I find myself wondering how he spends his Christmas, what he's doing right now, when I'll be able to see him again. I feel a slight pang of guilt that even after such a lovely day with Jonathan, when I'm feeling so close and in love, I'm still so easily distracted by thoughts of someone else.

Chapter 17

New Year's Eve comes around, and Jonathan and I are going out for a fancy meal. I'm hoping it'll be like our pretend date and we'll have an amazing time, reminiscing about old times. I'm wearing a sequinned party dress and I feel incredible. I spent ages getting ready, taking a series of photos of myself which I've sent to Ben in backwards order, a virtual striptease from fully dressed up in heels and makeup, down to just underwear and then completely naked, but for the heels.

Holy shit! I can't wait to see you again soon. Happy New Year! comes the response from Ben, sending my heart racing with anticipation.

His positive reaction has made me determined to strip in real life for Jonathan later. I've only thought about doing this once before, on his 21st birthday. I got all dressed up and everything, but he just wasn't into it. It was horrible; I felt disgusting and unwanted. I'm hoping tonight will be different, that it'll blow his mind, though I'm prepared for it to be totally embarrassing too. Fingers crossed; a few champagnes might give me the confidence I need to go through with it.

Over dinner we have the obligatory conversation about new

year's resolutions, and I share that mine is to learn to change a tyre. We both decide we should start exercising more: he settles on cycling, whilst I choose running. I enjoyed going out for that run before I met Ben and have been a couple of times since and can already feel it getting easier.

"When I'm running, it gives me good thinking time, helps me work out all this opening up stuff in my head."

Jonathan gets a forlorn look on his face. "I was hoping you might change your mind about all that now that you've had sex with someone else, that you might've got it out of your system."

I let out a sharp, exasperated breath, my head falling into my hands. "But I had a really amazing time. Why wouldn't I want to do that again? You want us to have this freedom but never actually use it?"

"I suppose so. I don't want to take your freedom from you, and I do want that freedom too, but I wish you'd choose not to use it, that a bit of harmless flirting once in a while would be enough. I never thought it would go this far."

I wish I could stop wanting this, to take it all away and be the monogamous girlfriend he wants and deserves. But I am who I am, and this desire for more isn't going away just yet.

"You've let it go this far though. I made it clear what I wanted right from the start. Why didn't you say no, shut it down before it got to this point? You just don't take me seriously anymore. Did you think I was just trying to get your attention? Christ! Maybe I was. Maybe if you weren't so wrapped up in work and doing up the house, you might notice I exist and actually spend some time with me."

I'm getting too worked up. He gazes down at the table, fiddling with his fork. "Do we really have to talk about this tonight?" He looks sad and downtrodden, his voice quiet. I don't want to make him feel like this. But I can't let it go now that he's finally talking to me, engaging in this conversation I've been waiting so long to have.

"You don't want to talk about it any other time, so tonight seems as good as ever to me."

And just like that, our nice New Year's date night is ruined by arguing. Twenty-fourteen is off to a bang all right. We get the bill and leave before walking home silently in the cold, my crossed arms at least adding a little warmth to my body, all thoughts of a strip tease forgotten.

I storm straight to bed when we get home and lie there seething. Jonathan climbs in next to me but doesn't make any attempt to touch me or talk to me. He must be able to sense that I'm awake. I want to touch him or talk to him, even just roll over to face him, but I can't make myself do it. He's right there next to me, but the bed might as well be a thousand miles wide.

Chapter 18

I'm distracted at work all week that I can't concentrate on anything properly. I'm worried Jonathan is never going to be okay with any of this, just as I'm discovering how amazing it is. Better than I could've even anticipated. I don't know what I'll do if he says it all has to stop. Do I want it enough to leave him so I can continue exploring by myself? Am I brave enough to do that? I think I'd regret it; I do know how good I've got it with him, and surely there are worse things than being bored? But if we stay together without it, would he ever truly be able to trust me again? Could I trust myself?

It's really quiet in the café after the hustle and bustle of December, and everyone has that post-Christmas January gloom so I can get away with being a bit distracted, but Julie is going to fire me soon if I keep this up.

Julie's daughter, Jo, comes in wrapped up like a snowman in hat, scarf, gloves, boots, and coat. She pulls off her hat to reveal dodgy, stripy highlights straight out of the Nineties. She must've done these herself; no hairdresser would do that to someone anymore. I can't quite read her expression—it's a little apprehensive, I think.

"Sorry, Jo, your mum's not here today."

"It's you I've come to see."

Me? Has something happened to Julie?

She tilts her head to one side, and a real look of concern and pity takes over her face as she tells me very slowly and quietly, and a little overdramatically, "Sophie, I'm really sorry. I was on a dating app and I'm sure I saw your boyfriend on it. Would you like me to show you?"

I have to stifle a relieved laugh at this. I don't want her to think I'm not appreciative of her honesty; she didn't have to tell me. "It's okay. I know he's on there. We're doing an open thing. But it's really sweet of you to tell me, thank you. I hope you'll understand why I'd rather you didn't mention this to your mum?"

Her face is easier to read now. It's not relief. It's disappointment. Disappointment that her news hasn't had the dramatic impact she expected, that she hasn't got herself a nice, juicy piece of gossip.

I hope she doesn't tell Julie. If this is how her daughter reacts, I can't imagine she'd be on board. I want—need—to keep Julie on side. It doesn't matter how often I talk about quitting, getting a "real" job elsewhere. I know I'm not going to do it. I've got it too easy. I like the hours, it's good fun, the customers are all lovely, and I get to eat whatever I want for lunch every day. Julie is a great boss, and I need to buck my ideas up to show her I know that and appreciate her and the job.

Things are still a little tense with Jonathan after our New Year's fight and now I'm again desperately hoping we'll be just like Frank and Ethel, or my parents, one day. How can I make things better with and for Jonathan without giving up what I need for myself? I'm scared I've thrown it away all for just a shag. Scared what they'd all think of me if they knew.

Ethel pulls me from my thoughts as she comes up to pay—the first time she's ever done so. Frank is far too much of an old-fashioned gentleman to let her deal with the money usually. That's when I notice the stick next to his chair. I'm sure I've not seen him with a stick before. He must've had a fall or something.

"Six pounds fifty please," I say with my sweetest of smiles.

She looks down into her hands, in which she holds a five-pound note, a pound coin, and a fifty-pence piece, and then stares back at me blankly.

I smile at her patiently and she seems to come round, passing me the money.

I follow her to the table under the pretence of clearing their cups away so I can check in with Frank. "Are you okay?" I ask, glancing at his stick.

"Oh yes, dear, I had a little fall and now the doctors are making me use this thing for a few weeks so it doesn't happen again, but I don't need it really."

I help Ethel into her coat as Frank gets up, and then walk them both to the door, waving them off with a smile.

"I'm seeing Sarah again tomorrow," Jonathan announces out of nowhere the moment I get home from work. I didn't even know they were still in touch. I'm glad they are, but the secrecy of it is a little unnerving, almost as if they think they've been doing something wrong.

Have they? What would that even mean in this situation?

"I thought you didn't fancy her."

"I'm allowed to change my mind."

And that's that. He's going on a second date.

Chapter 19

A cold sweat appears on my brow when I hear Jonathan come in the door after his second date with Sarah. I don't know what I'm so bloody nervous about. I stand at the sink, staring out of the window, unconvincingly pretending I'm too focused on scrubbing the frying pan to have noticed he's come in.

As he stands behind me, I can barely breathe.

Suddenly his hands are at my waist. With one hand, he reaches for his cock in his jeans whilst the other teases my pussy through my leggings. It's been so long that I'm wet almost instantly, my breath shallow and heart racing as he tears them off, along with my underwear, pushes his cock into me and fucks me rough and hard against the sink.

He comes quickly and slowly pulls my leggings back up for me, his tongue leading its path up my leg.

I turn to look at him, a sheen of sweat on his face, cock still out, and lean in to kiss him. "I'm sorry."

"Me too."

Apparently an afternoon of Sarah listening to Jonathan whining about me was enough to put any thoughts of a sexual nature out of her head, and instead they've become friends. She listened to him, gave him the time he needed to talk through what happened and how it felt, things I wish he could say to me but know he can't. He needed this. After he told Chris about the kiss, he felt judged for not breaking up with me and hasn't spoken to him since, and I don't think he's spoken to anyone else about it at all. Sarah might just be responsible for saving us.

We agree this is uncharted territory. It's okay that he finds it difficult; it's early days. Jonathan isn't sure he wants anything to do with opening up right now. He thinks he's meant to be monogamous. He can see how invigorated it's made me, though, and encourages me to make another date with Ben if I want to, but makes it clear he doesn't want to know any details about it when it happens.

I don't need to be told twice. I text Ben and arrange to see him again. At his house again. I realise I've set the tone by going straight there, that he's not going to waste his time and money wooing me on dates. But that's okay. Whatever I might've hoped for, I'm not going there for the conversation. In fact, I quite like how upfront it all is, no mind games.

I run four times in a week and have homemade soup for lunch every day in preparation for our second date. I feel on top of the world. I'm not sure how much of it is me trying to lose weight for him, or whether I'm just more energised and motivated because I'm excited. Either way, I'm healthier. That's got to be a good thing.

Half of me is wondering what I'm doing; feeling guilty, selfish, and greedy for putting a good relationship in harm's way, hurting a good man who loves me and cares for me. Am I gaslighting him by telling him this is normal and that he should be okay with it when everything else in the world is telling him otherwise?

Since talking with Sarah, Jonathan seems motivated in a way he didn't before. They're talking about going cycling together, and he's even thinking about going for a Head of Year promotion at work. I buy Jonathan a present: a cycling top. I'm hoping it'll help him to follow through with his new year's resolution; and encourage him to see more of Sarah too.

It was a good decision. He's thrilled with his top and straight on the phone to his parents to arrange to collect his bike from their garage, where it's sat idle for years.

Chapter 20

I *want to tie you up tonight.*

Ben's text comes out of the blue, at work the morning of our second date. I feel a little spasm in my pants as I read it, my face instantly flushing at the thought of it. It's like everyone in the café knows about it. I sneak off to the toilet to reply and take a minute to compose myself.

I've never done anything like that before, I reply.

Do you want to try?

Do I? The thought of it terrifies and excites me. I know it would never work with Jonathan. We'd get it wrong somehow or just feel too stupid. But with Ben, I just know it'll be amazing. *Yes please.*

Awesome! Let me know what your boundaries are so I don't do anything you're not comfortable with.

We have to use a condom, and I'm not allowed to do anal. And nothing in my own house, but that's okay as I'm coming to yours anyway!

No, not Jonathan's rules. Your boundaries.

What are my boundaries? I don't know! I've never pushed my sexual boundaries hard enough (or at all) to know where they lie. I stare at my phone in silence, not knowing how to respond to this but feeling confident that if he's asked me this question it must mean he knows what he's doing.

I'm not sure. Can I just let you know if I don't like something?

Okay. Can't wait to see you later!

* * *

Walking up to his door this time, I'm even more nervous than before, not knowing quite what to expect, worried my expectations are too high. I arrive, and he kisses me, his lips a little chapped and rough against mine. His hand touches my back, sending a jolt of electricity up my spine. I melt, all thoughts of fear and guilt gone from my head because it just feels so right. A primal instinct takes over: this is what I was put on this Earth to do.

He takes my hand and silently leads me upstairs to his bedroom, which is as stark as his lounge—plain white walls, plain navy bedding, a simple mirror and lamp, a large pine wardrobe (perhaps the chaos is hidden within there?).

He barks, "Take your clothes off."

Obediently, I strip. I feel a bit silly, like I'm in a play. I almost want to laugh but I know it will ruin the moment.

"Stand facing the wall."

I stand there, completely naked, hands high up pressing into the wall, back arched so my ass sticks out for him. He's still fully dressed, and I can't see him but I can feel his eyes appraising me. I still feel slightly ridiculous, but sensing him taking in every part of my body is sending my pussy wild, the uncertainty of what might happen next doing the same to my brain. He strokes my hair before gathering it together to pull my head around to kiss me.

86

The world slips away. I'm spellbound.

"Get on all fours on the bed."

I comply, looking out of the window at the garden outside, the last of the day's sun shining on my face. The sting of a slap on my ass catches me off guard. He starts gently but the slaps get harder and harder as he can see how much I like it, eventually so hard that it takes my breath away. It hurts, but I like it; pain is different in this context.

He rolls me onto my back. "Hands above your head." He ties my hands together on his headboard, and I look up into those gorgeous hazel eyes. I'm fully in the moment now. It's not ridiculous anymore, it's just hot. "Do you want me to fuck you?"

"Yes!" I reply eagerly, breathless.

"Beg me."

"Please fuck me. I want you so bad. Please."

Finally, his clothes come off, his cock a pleasant arrival to our party. He pushes my knees up to my shoulders and pounds me hard. I'm helpless, absolutely at his mercy. I can barely move, but it's amazing to be under his powerful spell like this, free of any kind of responsibility to make the right next move.

"God, I love fucking you," he shouts, and I can hear how out of breath he is.

Fuck! No one has ever said anything like that to me before, and certainly never so emphatically. I feel like I should say something back to reciprocate, but I don't have the guts to do it.

He kneels upright and pulls my feet up to his shoulders and looks at me, straight into my eyes, his chin jutting out in determination. He then moves his thumb to my exposed clit. I throw my head back in pleasure; it's almost too much for me, but I don't want him to stop. It feels like crying: breathless, uncontrollable, vulnerable, but oh-so freeing and satisfying, emptying me of all my worries.

I'm breathing hard as he moves his strong hand to my throat, setting off my orgasm.

I lie there, shaking, as he strokes me, touching every single inch of my tingling skin with his fingers and tongue and breath to prolong my orgasm even further, his soft touch all the more alluring after the hard, rough sex.

As I lie breathless and still shaking slightly, he kneels over me and finishes on my chest before rolling onto the bed next to me. He wipes me clean and unties my hands, and we rest there together, too tired and sweaty to touch or talk.

After a short recovery doze, we have some small talk about work, the weather, how our days have been, and then he starts talking about his ex-girlfriend again. He bumped into her yesterday in the supermarket with a guy he'd not seen before, and he isn't sure if it's her boyfriend or not. I guess that explains why he wanted to feel some control tonight. I know I'm supposed to find it uncomfortable or weird to have someone I've just had sex with talk about their ex, but I don't. Again, it just makes me feel closer to him and I like it. I know I can think of Ben straight after having sex with Jonathan, so it would be hypocritical of me to be offended by this.

"It sounds like you still really love her. How come you split up?" I ask.

He looks right into my eyes now for a moment, but averts his eyes before answering my question. "We wanted a baby. She had three miscarriages in one year. We've just been through too much. I think she sees me and is reminded of all that pain and disappointment, and she just can't take it."

When I look at him again, I can sense the depth of his sadness and I just want to take it all away for him. "I'm so sorry. That sounds awful for you both."

I cuddle into him, nuzzling my head into his shoulder. He lets out an involuntary sigh but then tenses up, like he's given away more than he intended to.

The comfortable atmosphere in the room changes and feels thicker now, more strained.

It's time for me to leave.

Chapter 21

Jonathan is better prepared when I return home this time. Following some advice Sarah gave him, he got some macho apocalyptic Brad Pitt action film lined up, along with a whole host of snacks to keep him company whilst I was out. When I get home, he doesn't seem angry or jealous or relieved. If anything, he's more annoyed I've interrupted his evening to himself.

We've agreed I should shower when I get in, to wash away any traces of someone else being on me.

Showered or not, Jonathan doesn't touch or kiss me over the next four days but is otherwise his normal loving self. I don't know what to make of this, and he's made it clear he doesn't want to talk about it. It's actually a relief, because I think I've got cystitis from not using the toilet straight after having sex with Ben, and I have bruises blossoming on my bum from where he spanked me, which somehow, I don't think Jonathan would like to see.

I wake up on the fifth morning with Jonathan spooning me, his morning wood nudging my lower back, and I take this to mean things are back to normal.

A week after seeing Ben, Lucy texts me asking if I fancy a

drink. But I don't. Instead, I ask if she'd like to go out for a run. It's a beautiful evening, the bright sunset glinting through the trees. Lucy is immaculate as ever in her expensive-looking matching running gear, hair tucked away inside a cap. My tatty old trainers and T-shirt seem even shabbier than normal beside her. But since trying to get fit for Ben, I've been doing more exercise and eating better than ever before, and it shows—I match her stride for stride.

We finish our run and stop to stretch in the park. Now that my breathing is calmer, I give her my latest update. "So, I met Ben again."

"How was it? Tell me everything!"

"It was fun. Kinky. He bossed me around and spanked me. I've never done any of that stuff before. I'm sure if Jonathan and I tried it together, we'd just laugh at each other, but Ben totally knew what he was doing. And he took it seriously, so I had to, as well."

"God, my sex life is so bloody boring! So, what's happening with him now? And how's Jonathan doing?"

"He's okay, I think. He was fine whilst I was out as far as I can tell. It's taken a few days of him not really touching me, but we've been getting on fine, and things seem to have gone back to normal."

I can't bring myself to tell her that Ben hasn't contacted me at all since that date. I miss his regular check-ins. I've tried searching for him on Facebook for clues as to what's going on with him, but I can't find him. I don't even know his surname.

I've pored over every moment of what happened, trying to work out what I did or said wrong, and come up with nothing. I tell myself he's just busy, he's boring anyway, he wasn't even that interested in getting to know me, he's rude, and who knows? Maybe he really did freak out that he liked me too much and couldn't handle it.

I'm far too scared to tell Jonathan that just as he's coming to terms with me seeing Ben, Ben doesn't want to see me anyway.

Chapter 22

L ucy comes into the steamy café with her girls, who are adorable in their matching raincoats and mismatched wellies—one yellow and one blue glittery welly each. They take their time peeling off their layers of hats, coats, and jumpers as they adjust to being indoors again. The weather is crazy at the moment; a whole section of sea wall has been washed away down in Devon, leaving train tracks hanging mid-air.

Eventually, Hannah and Freya settle down at the table and become engrossed in their hot chocolates, giving them their undivided attention. I've gone all out with a whipped cream mountain on each and topped them up with Maltesers and a flake. They're fully absorbed in the important task of trying not to waste a drop.

Wiping chocolate from her daughters' faces as they pack up to leave, Lucy looks at me seriously and asks me again, "Are things still okay with you and Jonathan?"

"Yes, it feels really good between us," I tell her as I pull out my too-tight hairband with a grimace and redo my ponytail.

And this time I'm sure, so long as he doesn't have to hear about it at least. Things are easier now we're actually doing it rather than having endless conversations and worrying about all the hypothetical outcomes. I know he's given up on the idea of finding another partner for himself. He's just not that way inclined. I know he wishes I'd come to the same conclusion too, but he accepts I'm not there yet and that I might never get there.

Although I'm sure he'd be glad to hear it, I still don't tell Jonathan just yet that Ben seems to have ghosted me. I think he'd judge Ben and question my choices for sleeping with someone who'd do that. At what point do I decide he's fully ghosted me and isn't just busy with his life anyway? I'm not even entirely sure I'll be able to say no if he reappears and invites me over again.

Things seem good between me and Jonathan this time; I think he's taking it all in stride. I hope he'll keep seeing Sarah; he seems much happier now than he has in months.

Valentine's Day is coming up soon, so we're decorating the café again, a red carnation on each table, heart-shaped shortcake biscuits, pink bunting in the windows. We may have gone a little overboard—it feels like Madam Puddifoot's café in Harry Potter, a sickly-sweet explosion of bows and bunting and hearts and flowers.

It's just Frank and Ethel in the café one cold drizzly afternoon, so I ask if she'd like to help decorate some biscuits again after she enjoyed it so much at Christmas, although I'm not entirely sure if it was the decorating or being around children she liked more. She beams up at me at the suggestion, and so does Frank. Before we know it, she's singing away to herself as she's lost in her own world, turning the heart-shaped biscuits baby pink.

Frank has that same expression on his face, content to

watch her and pleased to see her so happy, but with a quiet thoughtfulness lurking in the background that I can't quite put my finger on. I sit down with them.

"You used to love cooking, didn't you, love?" He looks at me with a smile. "She was never happier than when she was in the kitchen baking a cake for the boys to come home to after school or after they'd worn themselves out running around, making dens, and riding their bikes and whatever other mischief they used to get up to that I'd probably rather not know about."

"Does she do much cooking anymore?"

"Not really. We just get microwave meals now or eat simple things that don't take too much work. I help a lot more these days than I used to, so we need to keep it simple! I think she misses it, but I'm not sure it would be safe having her around all those heavy pans and boiling water and big knives now. Apart from anything else, she'd get too tired standing."

Normally for Jonathan's birthday, I buy him a chocolate cake from the Co-op, a running joke just like my coconut one. But for Valentine's Day—a day that usually passes us by like any other—inspired by Ethel's love of cooking, this year I decide to make him a red velvet cake, thick with cream cheese icing. I enjoy the ritual, weighing the butter and sugar, whisking them together, adding eggs and colouring, folding in the flour, thoroughly licking the bowl once the cake is safely in the oven, and filling the house with the irresistible and comforting smell of baking.

Valentine's Day passes without any contact from Ben, and this gives me some closure. I know he's gone for good now. I feel relieved to have clarity, to not feel like I'm waiting or hoping to hear from him anymore.

I tell myself I'm disappointed and confused that he's ghosted me, but grateful to have had two incredible experiences that will stay with me forever. Whenever I find myself feeling a bit low, pining for him, even just one of his cute messages, I repeat like a mantra, *I'm disappointed but grateful. I'm disappointed but grateful.*

It works. I'm disappointed but grateful. I'm not sad and I'm not angry. He doesn't owe me anything—we only met twice! I refuse to let myself feel any kind of heartbreak over this.

Chapter 23

A week later, in the pub with a bottle of red between us, Amy gives me her latest romantic news update. "I downloaded that app you were telling me about at Christmas, where you met Ben. I've started seeing this guy, Matt. He's amazing!"

She goes on to tell me all about Matt and she's so animated and happy, her old self. I haven't seen her like this in over a year, since her big breakup. I'm so happy for her that I'm smiling as much as she is.

She asks about Ben, and I tell her I don't think I'll see him again.

"Well, let's get you back on the app then!"

Giggling like the pair of schoolgirls we once were, together we take a look at who's on there. Before long, I've matched with Patrick. Unlike Ben, he's ten years older than me, his dark curls and short beard showing the tiniest hint of silver. His piercing blue eyes stare out at me from my phone screen. He's married and has children, which is new and intriguing.

Patrick and I have been messaging every day, several times a day, for the past week. A jolt of excitement rushes through my body every time my phone beeps; my smile wide when his name pops up, disappointed if it's anyone else. He tells me about his wife Kate and their kids Ruby and Max, and he asks me about my relationship, and my life. We talk about his work as a photographer, what we're watching on TV, what music we're listening to. There's an undertone of flirtation behind it all, but it feels very adult. I *like* it.

I'm still not really sure where Jonathan is with everything, so I emphasise to Patrick how busy I am, to put off any talk of meeting too soon.

At last, I tell Jonathan about Ben ghosting me, but that he can't celebrate for too long, no time for I-told-you-so, because I've started messaging someone else and I'd like to meet him.

"This is a lot to take in at once. I don't understand why you didn't tell me about Ben before now?"

"I wasn't completely sure if he had ghosted me or not, so I wasn't sure how to bring it up. I thought maybe he was just busy or something."

Jonathan looks patronisingly sympathetic. Did I really think that?

"That's not true. I mean...I was sure. I was embarrassed about it."

"I knew something was up with you. You've been quiet. I was worried it was me, that you were going to finish with me or something."

I bring my eyes to his and see him smiling back at me with such love and I suppose perhaps some relief I'm not leaving him.

"If you're feeling sad about anything, I want you to tell me about it. Even though I might not have liked you being with Ben, it still makes me sad that you're sad. It's my job to help you feel better."

I cuddle into Jonathan, glad this is all out in the open and that he's on my side, here to support me, unconditionally.

We leave it at that for now—he knows I'd like to meet Patrick, but I've not strictly asked to yet.

He meets Sarah for a drink, and I don't know quite what she says, but she encourages him to let me arrange a date. I owe Sarah a lot! I'd be intrigued to meet her, but Jonathan seems to like keeping us separate. I wonder what he's telling her that he's not telling me.

We talk more, and agree to a new *No Sex On First Dates* rule, which seems to make Jonathan feel more comfortable. I'm not against it, sure it'll make me appear more mature for Patrick, who I immediately tell about this agreement so he can set his expectations in the right place. It kind of sucks some of the excitement and anticipation out of it, but it's nice too, being so honest.

Patrick and I arrange to go on a real date, a meal in a nice restaurant. With the promise of a borrowed outfit, Amy and I have a fun afternoon trying on clothes in her bedroom. Everything in Amy's flat is pretty and colourful. Having never been influenced by sharing her space with a live-in boyfriend, the space is a girly haven. Piles of old fashion magazines on the floor, earrings, shoes, handbags and jackets seem purposefully on display rather than just not put away properly. Even the old coffee cups on the floor are all pretty, the clumps of hair stuck to the shower wall a mark of her independence with no man telling her it's disgusting.

Amy is doing my makeup for me, using all of her high-quality makeup rather than my cheap rubbish.

"Okay, you can look now," says Amy with a satisfied smile,

pointing me toward the mirror.

I burst out laughing. "Amy! I look fucking ridiculous! I can't go out like this!"

She's done some admittedly beautiful and colourful eye-shadow, but it's way too much. Various shades of brown and gold reach all the way from my lashes up to my brows, and she's contoured my face Kardashian-style. It's trying way too hard, and I don't feel like myself.

"It looks great, but it's okay, I can do it again. I promise I'll be more subtle this time."

She hands me a face wipe and doesn't even seem annoyed as I remove all her work and expensive products. I think she might even be pleased she gets to do my makeup because it feels like we're teenagers all over again. I've missed this.

One very messed-up bedroom and a tummy full of butterflies later, and I'm all set: subtle makeup, denim jacket over a girly floaty floral dress with just a hint of cleavage, but an otherwise sensible outfit, the sort of thing I could wear for dinner with my parents. I want him to woo me, to treat me right, and for us to get to know each other properly. To set the scene so this doesn't just turn into a sex thing like it did with Ben. Amy has even done my hair for me—gentle waves flowing down my back like a mermaid.

"You look great! How are you feeling?"

"Nervous." I'm too embarrassed to tell her I'm actually more nervous I won't fancy him than that he won't fancy me. Even though Ben has ghosted me, he also did wonders for my confidence. And I've still got Jonathan, so I've got nothing to lose by putting myself out there.

"Don't worry about it. You'll be fine."

The most experienced dater I know, Amy goes on to give me

lots of complicated tips for the date, all of which go in one ear and out the other, until she deems me ready to go. I'm coming back to hers later to fill her in on all the gory details, to get the full measure of my excitement out first, hoping this will give Jonathan time to process whatever feelings he has this evening.

Chapter 24

In all my excitement and inexperience, I forget all about being fashionably late and arrive first. I order and pay for a bottle of wine with two glasses. Although I want to be wooed and treated like a lady, I also want to show him what an independent woman I am and that I don't expect him to pay for everything.

We're in a fancy restaurant I've never been to before, but I still have a little niggling worry in the back of my mind that someone will see me here with someone who isn't Jonathan. A smaller part of me actually wants to get spotted; it would be a bit of a thrill, and maybe even that all this could come out in the open and not have to feel so secretive anymore.

He arrives, tall like Jonathan but chunkier—I can already imagine feeling so safe held in his arms. I watch a smile emerge on his face as he spots me and walks over to the table.

"I'm so nervous," I blurt out immediately as my face starts to burn. I'm feeling like an embarrassed teenager. This isn't the first impression I planned on making.

He laughs and smiles at me, his whole face lighting up and eyes crinkling.

"You must be Sophie."

Putting my nervousness out there seems to relax us both our nerves, even if I'm going to be cringing about it forever.

We slip straight into conversation easily; we seem to have shared just enough by text to know what questions to ask each other without repeating things we already know. Unlike Ben talking about his ex in a way that (in hindsight, at least) felt a little uncomfortable, we both talk openly about our partners because they're part of our lives, and in the same way, a part of us. It feels so honest.

He tells me more about his work as a photographer for a magazine and occasionally doing some freelance work. It sounds like he gets to travel and go to all sorts of interesting places and events.

"Do you do much photography just for yourself, or has it lost its shine now you do it all the time for work?"

"Sometimes. I like to combine it with trips to new places, get the family out somewhere new and scout places for potential photoshoot locations and that sort of thing. The kids get annoyed with the early mornings when I want them to go and see a sunrise somewhere new, but once they're out, they love it. What's your work like?"

How much can I say about working in a café? It's times like this that I wish I had some dream I was working toward on the side to make up for still having the job of a teenager. "I love it. My boss is great, and it's really handy being so close to home and everything." I'm boring myself here—I can do better than this. "I've been getting to know this sweet couple recently. Frank and Ethel, they're called. They come in all the time and they're so in love with each other, it's adorable."

Frank and Ethel to the rescue! Patrick is leaning in and seems genuinely interested to know more about them and how I got to know them. Apparently, knowing them has turned my boring job and personality into something more interesting.

Several times I notice the poor waiter trying to make headway to take our order, but unable to find a suitable break in the conversation. I can see him there; I'm hungry and I know what I want to eat. I want to stop talking and order, but I'm so engrossed in listening to him that I can't.

Finally, we pause for breath long enough that the waiter can get to us, and we both order the butternut squash and spinach risotto—a meal I've chosen specifically because it feels safe in terms of risk of food poisoning, spillage, or any kind of difficulty eating. Jonathan has an annoying habit of scraping his knife loudly across the plate as he cuts his food, which makes my ears bleed...no risk of that with risotto!

"Are you vegetarian too, then?" I ask him.

He glances at me for a moment, deep in thought, like he's trying to work out his answer. I'm confused about what's so difficult about my question. Is he worried I'll change my mind if he says he eats meat?

He takes a breath and gives me a smile that doesn't quite reach his eyes.

"I'm trying to cut out all meat and dairy, or at least cut down. We all are. Kate's mum has bowel cancer. Her doctor says a diet change probably won't do anything for her now, but it could help the rest of us avoid getting it in the future. So we're doing it to show her mum support, and for ourselves too. And it has been hard, especially finding things the kids will eat, but I do feel better for it."

I don't really know what to do with this information, so I offer up a weak smile, which I hope comes across as reassuring. "I'm so sorry about her mum. That must be really hard."

"It is. But one of the worst things is feeling helpless. At least this feels like we're doing something a bit proactive."

I'm doing my best to keep a sombre expression on my face, but inside my heart is singing. He's told me something big and scary and real. He must trust me and like me!

The waiter returns with our food. "Would you like any parmesan on that?"

"No, thank you," we both say in unison with a little knowing smile at each other.

"How are your kids dealing with their grandma being sick? Do they understand what's happening?"

"They're okay. It's hard to know how much they really understand—they've never known anyone who died before. They're very close to Kate's parents. You know how it is with grandparents, it's all sweets and fun days out and never being shouted at or told to go to bed."

"It's nice they're close. I never really knew my grandparents. Dad's parents both died when I was really young, and I don't remember them at all. We saw Mum's occasionally, but Mum didn't really seem to want me spending time with them. I don't know why—she won't ever talk about it, but they just don't get on. I sort of felt like it was my fault and Mum resented me for it, but obviously I hadn't done anything, so I don't feel like that anymore. It was just part of my angry teenage phase, I think."

I don't know why I just told him that. I never talk about this with Jonathan. I worry I sound judgemental, and Jonathan will be defensive on Mum's behalf, or I worry he'll repeat something to Mum that she won't like. It's safer with Patrick—I'm not going to have to worry about him telling Mum anything he shouldn't, because they'll never meet.

We carry on chatting as we eat, and then just sit quietly gazing at each other across the table, smiling inanely. His sky-blue eyes have a darker blue outline and are almost green around the pupils, giving them an extra depth I hadn't appreciated through my phone screen. His teeth are a little crooked, the front two crossed over like mine were until I convinced Mum to let me have a brace. Maybe she was right that I needn't have bothered, because to me, his wonky teeth make him even more attractive. The food is delicious and I'm enjoying the conversation, but all I can think about is getting out of here and kissing that mouth.

The speed with which he gets the bill and pays after we've eaten suggests he's thinking along the same lines. Or perhaps after me buying the wine, he just really wants to show me that he's a true gentleman and is going to pay whether I like it or not.

"I want to kiss you," I say as we leave the restaurant.

He smiles and takes my hand but doesn't make a move, leaving me feeling a little embarrassed and confused. Maybe he's not interested, or maybe he's nervous and trying to pluck up the courage to do it, or maybe it's all a clever game designed to make me want him even more.

Before I can decide which it is, suddenly he's grabbed my shoulders, pushed me up against the wall, and he's kissing me hard but in a chaste, innocent sort of way. His hands have moved to my waist now. I'm breathless with desire. He pulls away, his lips just out of reach of mine. I can hear his breath, as heavy as mine. He's looking right at me and smiling as I crane my neck forward, wanting more, more, and more.

"It was lovely to meet you. I'd really like to see you again."

And with that, the date is finished. The kind of date I could tell my mum about (at least, I could if I were single). A stark contrast to the hot excitement I had with Ben, but that didn't turn out so well in the end. It's nice to be left wanting more, feeling a little frustrated but also hopeful for what's to come next time, glad he's made it clear he'd like there to be a next time. I like the idea that it'll probably always be like this, always a little frustrating and unsatisfying, but that's also what keeps it interesting, and stops it from getting boring.

Chapter 25

I walk with a spring in my step back to Amy's and snuggle into her cosy bed to tell her everything, gushing in a way I've learned not to with Jonathan. Grinning like the Cheshire cat, I'm as excited about Patrick as she is about Matt. It's good to be in the same place as her for once; I know she found it hard being single while I was happily cosied up with Jonathan, however fun her life might've seemed from the outside.

She barely gets a word in edgeways all night, but I can see her smiling too in recognition of that great post-date feeling, the anticipation of the second date, all the possible futures opening up before me.

"What's his wife like then?" she asks, which I take as permission to do what I've been thinking about but not yet done: an internet stalk.

Clearly very open with her life, it doesn't take long to find Kate's Facebook profile via Patrick's (which I visit often, although I haven't yet had the guts to add him as a friend). She's predictably gorgeous in an outdoorsy, natural way, a mane of shiny brown hair and rosy cheeks framing her happy smile, as are their kids: the perfect, happy little family. I don't know what I wanted or expected. I'm glad she looks nice. It gives me faith that he must be a good guy if she's chosen him, but I can't help comparing myself to her. Why would he be interested in me when he already has someone as lovely as her?

I wish I'd never gone on her profile now, or at least that I'd done it alone so I could feel a bit pathetic and sorry for myself on my own.

I wake up horny at Amy's the morning after meeting Patrick and leave her still cosy and half asleep in her bed. I'm desperate to get back to Jonathan, to see how he is and to let him (hopefully, if he wants) reap the benefits of Patrick's attentions.

He's engrossed in Match of the Day, a big mug of coffee steaming by his side. He seems surprised to see me. "I wasn't expecting you back so early! How was your night?"

"It was nice. He was really lovely, and gentlemanly. I think you'd approve. We had a kiss and I hope I'll get to see him again."

"And that's really all? You stayed at Amy's? You didn't go back to his or anything?"

"I promise. How were you last night?"

"Honestly I was okay. I just kept myself busy and tried not to think about what you might be up to, and it was fine."

Without a word, I kneel on the floor, pull his cock out of his trousers, and take it in my mouth, feeling it grow as I lick and suck away with an enthusiasm I sometimes struggle to muster. I look up into his eyes as my tongue teases his swollen cock whilst my fingers are gently playing with his balls.

He lies back onto the sofa with a big sigh of pleasure, and my whole body relaxes in relief as I realise we really might actually make this all work.

Chapter 26

I'm woken up by the shrill ringtone of my phone. Lucy.

"Hi, are you okay?" I ask in a slightly panicked tone.

"Yeah, fine. You?"

"Oh. Yeah. Good, just not used to people phoning anymore unless it's an emergency!"

"Oh, sorry! It's early too, isn't it. I forget that everyone else doesn't get woken up at the crack of dawn. I just wondered if you wanted to come ice skating today. I promised the girls we'd go—they're obsessed with Frozen—but Dave can't come, and I don't think I can handle it on my own."

Two hours later, we edge onto the ice rink, Lucy and I dressed in warm layers, Hannah and Freya in matching Elsa dresses worn over woolly jumpers and thick tights. They're given big penguins to push around so they can't fall, whilst us adults are left to our own devices. Once they're feeling confident, Lucy and I decide to take it in turns to skate a few laps.

At first, I just wobble around the edge, holding on tight, whilst Lucy seems perfectly at home even on her very first lap. She's elegant and graceful, and she's fast! It's impressive to watch, and I have to keep pulling my attention back to the girls.

They ask to go around for a proper lap, and Freya chooses to take my hand instead of her mum's, making my heart burst. It's lovely going around listening to her chat away about preschool and her first wobbly tooth (she's very proud to have reached this milestone before Hannah) and it forces me to be a bit braver too.

We swap over, and this time I'm holding Hannah's hand as we go round and she tells me all about the beautiful bright white ice skates she wants to get for when she's a professional ice skater one day. I remember desperately wanting the same when I was younger, instead of the big, clumpy, uncomfortable plastic blue things we're all wearing now.

Afterwards, we take the girls to a playpark. It's an amazing park, all made from natural materials like wood and rope, unlike the brightly coloured metal climbing frames I remember. There's even a trampoline in the ground, which I'm having to hold myself back from jumping on. I feel like a part of their family, and it's nice visiting an alternate life for the day. After we've been pushing them on the swings for a while, Lucy sets the girls up on the slide so we can leave them to it and sit at one of the picnic tables.

"Oh! I got you something," says Lucy, reaching into her bag. She pulls out a black-and-white silk scrunchie and hands it to me. "For your hair. It's much kinder than those things you use."

"I love it! Thank you!" I tell her, putting my hair up immediately and using my phone camera as a mirror, while Lucy watches me with a slightly bemused look on her face.

"Where's Hannah gone?" she asks suddenly.

"We've only just sat down. She can't have gone far," I say, confused at how quickly Lucy has gone into panic mode when she's normally so calm and collected.

She storms over to Freya and demands, "Where's your sister?"

This sets Freya off crying, and I realise finding Hannah is going to be my job.

I take a good look around the park to see if I can spot her mass of hair, but she really is nowhere to be seen. I start to scour the park, heading straight for the slide and then to the secret tunnel under the fort, but I can't see her anywhere.

I'm panicking now, heart racing, eyes flitting around every-where, trying to take everything in at once. I can't even begin to imagine how Lucy must be feeling. I can't see her or Freya anywhere, so I assume they're still searching elsewhere in the playpark, or maybe outside of the park.

As I scan the outskirts of the park, I notice a bush move and walk toward it. "Hannah?"

The bush rustles again, and out she comes with a huge smile on her face.

"Are you okay? We've been looking for you."

She gazes up at me dreamily. "There was a butterfly. I was following it."

I take her hand and walk back to the picnic table. Lucy and Freya are back now. Lucy appears to be holding back tears and anger as she grabs Hannah by the shoulders and demands to know where she's been. All this attention seems to have thrown Hannah, who immediately starts crying.

"She's ok. She followed a butterfly into the bushes," I tell Lucy.

It's almost like I can see the rush of relief flow out of Lucy's body as her shoulders and everything about her relaxes. "Oh, my lovely girls! You scared me!" Lucy says, pulling Freya into her arms so they're having a big group hug.

It's so beautiful seeing the unconditional love for her girls pouring out of Lucy by the bucketful, but it just highlights to me how stressful and emotional parenting really is. I'm not sure I'd ever be cut out for it.

Lucy decides that's enough excitement for one day and that it's time to go home. As we make our way out of the park, Lucy laughs and fills me in on her search for Hannah. "You won't believe what I did. I saw a man and asked him if he'd seen my daughter. I just pointed at Freya and says she looks just like her. It was only as the words were leaving my mouth that I noticed his guide dog—he was blind! He was lovely about it, but I was too embarrassed to ask anyone else for help after that!"

* * *

Knowing Patrick's mother-in-law is sick prompts me to finally arrange to visit my parents for Mum's birthday, a phone call in which Mum isn't able to supress her surprise or excitement, and one that fills me with guilt.

It's torture not getting a second date whilst Patrick is focusing on supporting Kate. Desperate to see him again, I'm a fizzing ball of anticipation and frustration. But it's good to slow down too, for Jonathan to have some time to get his head around everything. I just want that next date booked in, something to look forward to, some certainty that he wants me and wants to see me again. Although, as I constantly repeat to Jonathan, this is all about the buzz and adventure that only comes with uncertainty.

Patrick and I video chat instead, lying in bed chatting away about once a week. I could talk to him for hours about anything and everything. I tell him more about my work, about Frank and Ethel, and about Tom and my parents. He tells me how hard it is seeing Kate so sad caring for her mum, how he doesn't feel like he can be upset too because he needs to be strong for her and the kids, how it's hard juggling all the extra things that need doing, how confusing it is seeing her smile and laugh with her friends when she seems so miserable around him. Telling me about it seems to help him, and that boosts me too. I come away from those calls aglow, sparkly, like I'm floating.

We usually keep it pretty clean, but I'm getting frustrated. I'm really horny. So, one day I call him out of the blue, completely naked. The camera is just on my face at first and I go straight into flirty mode, biting my lip, playing with my hair, and gradually moving my phone further away from me to hint at my nakedness. His eyes light up as he realises, and he rushes to his bedroom to get comfortable.

As soon as he's set up, eyes wide, I start to play. The camera is on my face and chest, but he can see my arm moving as I touch myself.

Softly, he describes what he'll do when we finally find ourselves naked together. "If I were there, I'd be kissing inside your thighs, pushing your legs apart..."

I move my hand faster and my breathing changes, heat spreading across my chest as I get more and more into it.

"Can I see what you're doing?"

I stop and think about it. Why would he want to see down there? I can barely bring myself to say the word vulva, even to myself, let alone have it bared on screen. I'd much rather his eyes were on my chest, boobs bouncing, nipples hard and wet with an open mouth in sight.

I want to please him, though, and to push myself to try new

things. I take a deep breath and move my phone down my body, struggling at first to find a good angle that's comfortable for my hand. Soon he can see my fingers pushing inside myself, stroking my clit.

"Oh, you're beautiful. I can't wait to touch you. I just want to eat you all up. Do you have any toys?"

Fully in the moment now, self-consciousness out the window, I reach for my vibrator, turn it on, and push it deep inside.

"Fuck!"

Chapter 27

Things have been really good with Jonathan since my date with Patrick. I think he likes that we had a proper old-fashioned date, taking things slow and not having sex. Between phone calls, I send Patrick naughty pictures and ask him for requests, which he's only too happy to give. Jonathan seems okay with anything virtual. It's the physical stuff he finds difficult to get his head around. So occasionally I'll ask him to help me get a picture just right, and then he cashes in too—I wouldn't bother getting dressed up and posing like that normally and I've never sent him a picture like that before, but now I see myself in a new, sexier light and I do it all the time.

It's not all dirty talk and pictures, though, not like it was with Ben. I want to tell Patrick all about my life, the little things that happen each day, and I want to hear about his too. I want him to be part of my life and I want to be part of his. With Ben, it was a bit more sordid, something I'd have wanted to keep at an arm's length. I like being open to all sorts of relationships and connections, just seeing how things develop with each person, not looking for anything specific and then being disappointed when I don't get it.

Patrick and Kate have the same rule as us about not bringing people to their house—especially since they have children there. I like the symmetry of us both being in a relationship. It feels more equal than it did with Ben. I'm not worried he'll get too attached, or that he'll meet someone who stops him from seeing me. And whilst I'm worried I might like him too much and will get too attached myself, be too much, too needy, being with Jonathan and having to go at his pace makes it easier to appear to play it cool, even if I don't feel very cool.

Lucy and I are out on one of our runs when I see him in the park. Ben. Sitting and laughing with who I choose to assume is his ex-girlfriend. I look at him as closely as I can without making a scene and wonder what I saw in him that made me quite so gooey-eyed. He's hot for sure, but not like I remember. He seems happy, though. I'm glad they've worked things out. And if it's not his ex, I'm happy he's met someone else who makes him smile like that. And I'm pleased for her too—she's in for a treat!

I don't point him out to Lucy. Instead, I tell her all about Patrick, about the photos I've been sending him and how good they've made me feel.

"I could never do that, not since having kids. My body is ruined," says Lucy, running next to me, looking incredible in her skin-tight clothing. She looks and smells great even after a run, when I'm a horrible, sweaty, red mess.

A mean little voice inside me tells me that's something I have over Kate at least: my body hasn't been stretched by pregnancy and childbirth. I wish it were something else, something I have rather than something I don't. I wish I was prettier or funnier or more intelligent, but younger and childless is about all I have on my side right now.

I run ahead a little to pull myself up out of this train of thought, telling myself that if I'm worried she's better than me, or I'm not good enough, then I should make myself better, not put her down.

I can't believe I'm jealous of his wife—it's ridiculous. Of course he loves her! I have to remind myself that him liking me and him liking her aren't mutually exclusive. That I like him a lot and I definitely, deeply love Jonathan, so I know in my head and in my heart that this is completely possible. The more I think about it, the more I realise it's a compliment—even though he has Kate, he still wants me too. I just need to know that he does like me, not that he doesn't like anyone else. I don't need or want to be his one and only.

Chapter 28

Jonathan is seeing Sarah a lot now. They've started cycling together, three or four times a week when they can. He's talked about getting back on his bike again for years, but this is the first time he's actually done anything about it. I'm pleased. I hate cycling and this gives me some time to myself. They've signed up to do a race together somewhere in the New Forest, so they're training hard. I barely see him anymore, but I'm enjoying the time on my own. Sarah is definitely doing Jonathan good. The cycling energises him and he seems to be coming around to all of this better than before, now he's got someone to talk to. I'm glad it's made him less obsessive about doing jobs around the house too; I don't miss the sounds of drilling and hammering one bit. The house is a much calmer place to be, even if it still isn't "finished."

On one of my quiet days to myself whilst Jonathan is out cycling, I realise I haven't heard from Amy for a while. Not unusual for Amy, but we've been seeing each other a lot more recently. My head has been full of Patrick, and I assume she's been busy with Matt too, so I'm not worried, but I do miss her.

I decide to call rather than text Amy. It rings and rings and rings.

When I still haven't heard from her an hour later, I set out to find her. Outside her flat, I ring the buzzer and wait.

"Hello?" comes her groggy voice over the telecom.

"Amy, it's Sophie. Are you okay?"

She doesn't answer me, but buzzes me in.

Two minutes later, I push open the door to her flat. Although always a bit of a mess, it feels different today, more neglected than usual, a dead bunch of flowers still in their vase, which all the water has evaporated from, the smell of the black bananas in her fruit bowl overpowering anything else in the flat. "Amy? Where are you?"

"In here."

I follow her croaky voice to her bedroom, where I find her in bed, hair a mess, old makeup on her face, still in pyjamas at two p.m. This isn't the Amy I know and love.

I take off my shoes and climb into the bed next to her.

I look at her, and her tears start streaming from her big green eyes. I snuggle into her, and we lie there like that, her silently crying for as long as she needs.

"Matt's married," she finally announces.

"Oh."

"His wife found pictures of me on his phone and hit the roof. He thinks they'll work it out, but he still wants to keep seeing me too. I don't know what to do."

"What do you want to happen?"

"I just wish she hadn't found out, or at least that he hadn't told me about it. I wish we could go back to how things were. I just want to be with him again and not have to feel guilty about it. I want him to leave her."

"Has he said he would leave her?"

"No. He's at least being honest about that. He'll never leave her. And she's not going to be letting him out of her sight now she knows about me."

I cuddle her a little tighter and realise I have tears in my eyes too. I wanted her to find happiness with Matt as much as I know she wanted it for herself. "You have to end it. He's married and he lied about it. Even if he left her, you could never trust him."

"Patrick's married."

"It's not the same. His wife knows. She has other partners too. It's open and honest—there are no lies there."

With that, I realise I'm taking his word for it. I trust him but I want to be sure. I need to meet Kate. He's been quieter recently. I assume he's busy with work and with his kids, and of course Kate's mum may have got worse...but what if it's really because she doesn't know and wouldn't like it if she did? He's made it clear he likes me and is keen to meet again, and of course he has to prioritise his family, but I find myself pining for him anyway, feeling a bit pathetic.

I don't feel like I can talk to Jonathan, or Lucy or Amy, because they'll tell me it's not worth the hassle—I have a lovely boyfriend, so why am I putting myself (and him) through this? Why can't I just be happy with what I've got? Keeping it to myself sends me in a downward spiral of sadness, beating myself up for being greedy and not content with my lovely boyfriend like a normal person would be. Don't I know how lucky I am?

As I walk home from Amy's, I work through it in my head. The rules are different here. Patrick isn't my husband; I'm not his girlfriend. I'm not looking for the perfect partner to meet my every desire and need. He's not my top priority, and I'm not his. If he was prioritising me over his wife and children, he wouldn't be the kind of person I'd want a relationship with anyway. This should all be joy and fun. And if I was getting what I wanted all the time, well, I'd probably stop wanting it, wouldn't I? Half the fun is the game, the anticipation, and the wanting.

I realise it's more like what I have with Amy. If I don't hear from her for a while, I don't automatically convince myself she hates me and I'll never hear from her again. Our relationship will ebb and flow over time; sometimes we see each other all the time, tell each other everything. Other times we'll go months without contact, confident we'll pick up where we left off next time we meet. I realise that, unless one of us does something awful, Patrick and I will never really have to break up. Even if we meet someone perfect and wonderful, a soulmate, that doesn't mean we'll have to make a choice or stop seeing each other.

It just might mean our relationship changes, that we see each other less often, or maybe become platonic.

Chapter 29

Sitting in the car as we drive up to visit my parents for Mum's birthday, singing emphatically along to Pharrell Williams' *"Happy"* like a pair of Minions, I receive a message from Patrick: *Kate's taken Ruby and Max to her mum's for the night tonight. Do you want to get a hotel or something? My treat.*

It feels like a kick to the stomach, getting a message like that—the message I've been longing for, but unable to say yes to seeing him. I'm gutted I can't meet him, annoyed at him for not knowing Kate would be away and not asking me sooner. But part of me is also glad this will show him I'm not available at his beck and call whenever he wants me. I hope it might make him put more effort into making time for me in future. And realistically I know Jonathan couldn't handle the spontaneity; he needs time to get used to the idea of me seeing someone else before I just go off and do it. We're still a way off from the levels of freedom I'm hoping for.

I can't, sorry, it's my mum's birthday.

At my parents' house, I have a crisis of confidence. I'm scared to leave my phone anywhere in case a message pops up from Patrick and they think I'm cheating on Jonathan. Do I really want to live like this? Maybe it isn't worth it after all. Watching Frank and Ethel these last few months and knowing Kate's mum is sick has made me more appreciative of my own family. I might not visit often but I do like knowing they're there, and I know I shouldn't take them for granted.

My parents probably would be understanding, but it's still not a conversation I want to have, not whilst I'm not even sure what I'd be telling them. So far, I've had two random, drunk, one-off kisses, a two-night stand, and one date. It really sounds more greedy-slut-trying-to-have-her-cake-and-eat-it-too than the wholesome, loving thing I have in mind, where they should be pleased I have extra people in my life who love and care for me. Surely all anyone wants to know is that their children are loved, and the more people loving them, the better, right? But I know it's not that simple in reality.

Mum is thrilled with her birthday present: a macaron cookery course for the two of us to do together soon. Macarons (or anything almond-based, really; Bakewell tarts and anything with marzipan are right up there too) are her absolute favourites and now she'll be able to make them whenever she wants. For the first time ever, I seem to have won on the present-buying stakes. This matches up to Tom's ridiculously expensive hamper of goodies (who in their right mind spends £30 on a bloody candle?). I've been enjoying helping Julie out more in the kitchen at work and want to learn to do more cooking, and it'll be nice to have some time with Mum outside of their house, where it always seems to feel a little tense.

Mum loved my present more than yours this year! I text Tom.

It's about time! How are you, sis?

I can't believe he's replied instantly! This isn't like him at all. He's usually far too busy and important for us. A wave of grief flushes through me as I realise just how much I miss my big brother. *I'm okay. Miss you. It's still weird being home without you. They've legalised gay marriage now, though. Maybe it's time to come home?*

Not likely! It's amazing out here. I don't think I could ever go back now.

Well, it was worth a try. I know he's never coming back for good, but I'd love him to just visit, or invite me to come and see him. I haven't seen him for three years now. *I've got to go. Dad's going to teach me to change a tyre!*

Good luck, sis xx

Whilst I'm here, I've decided to make good on my New Year's Resolution and ask Dad to teach me to change a tyre. I'm sure Jonathan and I would only end up arguing if he showed me—we learned that the hard way, trying to redo the kitchen when we first moved into our house. So I tend to stay out of the way with any and all DIY projects now and just leave him to it. Anyway, it'll be nice to have some time with Dad.

Dad shows me how to jack the car up to remove the wheel and then hands me the cold, heavy wrench to remove the wheel nuts. It's hard! It takes me quite a while, and I'm red and sweaty by the end of it, but eventually I get them all off, feeling even more grateful Jonathan was there to do this when we came up at Christmas in the cold.

Off comes the wheel, and Dad gives me a proper squeezy hug, like he's really proud of me. I don't remember the last time he hugged me or touched me at all, even when I was little. He never quite knew what to do with us when we were kids. I was a girl, and Tom was a boy, but not the kind of boy Dad could understand. He wasn't into sports, wasn't interested in helping out with Dad's various DIY projects around the house.

He was much happier reading quietly in his room or playing tea parties and dress-up with me. Then he came out, and I think he'd got himself so convinced himself that Dad would never be okay about it that he just took off for America almost immediately, with barely a backward glance. He never gave Dad a chance to come to terms with it and show him how much he loved him and accepted him. I was lost without him, my role model and playmate gone. The house never felt the same again without his smiling face, big laugh, and colourful outfits.

Dad lets go of me and starts coughing uncontrollably. I'm not sure whether he's trying to cover up feeling a bit emotional and awkward from our hug, or if his asthma is playing up. I pat him on the back a bit, but even this amount of contact seems strange.

Eventually his coughing settles.

"Are you okay, Dad? I heard you coughing a lot in the night too."

"I'm fine, I'm fine," he says dismissively.

"Have you been to the doctor?"

"I'm not going to the doctor. They never listen. I had it all the time when you were little and I was trying to get my back sorted. They didn't care how much pain I was in or that I couldn't sleep or go to work or provide for my family. They just wanted to know what painkillers I was taking or how much I was drinking. I wouldn't have needed to take the bloody painkillers if they'd just listened to me. Just leave it, will you?"

That's the longest speech I've heard from Dad in a long time and although I feel like I've pissed him off, it's nice to feel like he's opened up to me a bit. "Shall we get this thing back on then?" I say, changing the subject and wanting to get back to our nice moment, but sure I've ruined it.

Grumpily, he shows me how to put the wheel back on. I use all my strength to do it up as tightly as I can, terrified I'll get it wrong, visions of the wheel flying off on the motorway home flashing before my eyes.

Chapter 30

"So...whilst you were out messing around with the car with your dad, your mum asked me if you were pregnant!" Jonathan tells me on the drive home (all four wheels safely attached the whole way).

My mouth drops open, aghast. "What? But I've been doing all this running and eating better. I thought I'd lost weight! How can she possibly think I'm pregnant?" I slump in my chair, and Jonathan shakes his head, laughing at me.

"No, she said you were glowing, not fat!"

"Oh, well, I can't argue with that!"

He gets a gooey look in his eyes that I recognise from when we had our date night, and he's suddenly serious and soppy. "You are, you know. Glowing. I've never fancied you so much as I do lately. You seem much happier and more confident. It's sexy."

We're both smiling now; in fact, I feel like my whole body is smiling. I can't deny that I feel happier and healthier than I have in years, but I didn't realise it was so obvious from the outside. Any thoughts I'd had of giving Patrick up disappear as I realise all of this is doing me noticeable good, inside and out.

"Do you think we should have a baby?" I ask tentatively, not sure I'm ready to hear the answer.

"Do you want to?"

"No. There are too many people in the world already; I don't want to be part of the problem. And I saw how hard having kids was on my parents. I think I'm too selfish—I don't want to make my life harder than it needs to be. But I worry I'll look back and regret not doing it and it'll be too late to change our minds. And our parents would love it so much, wouldn't they? I do feel kind of guilty about it."

"It sounds like you've got more reasons to not do it than to do it, so that's good enough for me. And, if we do decide to go for it one day, it definitely shouldn't be out of guilt!"

"I know. But they've got more hope of me having a baby than Tom. Even if he did, he'd never visit anyway, so it would hardly matter. It might even be worse."

I spend the next few minutes gazing out of the window, wondering how on Earth I'm supposed to know if a decision is right or not. The decision to pursue this whole open-relationship thing even though I know it's so hard on Jonathan. The decision whether or not to have a baby. I think about seeing Lucy with her girls, that special, incomparable, unbreakable, unconditional loving bond they share, how they light each other up. Do I really never want that for myself?

The last time I had to make a decision this hard was when I decided not to go to university. I'd got all my offers through, got the A-Level results I needed, and was looking forward to it, but something made me change my mind. It just wasn't the right course or the right time or the right city. Part of me didn't want to put any extra pressure on my parents to pay for me to go. I'd already seen how supporting Tom through university had nearly broken them. I was happily with Jonathan, and he'd started a year before, so I do at least know he isn't to blame. Amy too—they'd both gone off to Sheffield (following the rise of the Arctic Monkeys and Pulp before them; Jonathan wanted to be around to see every new band he could, and Sheffield seemed the place to be at the time) and I'd had an offer there—we could've all lived together, had an amazing time.

Did I make the right decision back then? Most of the time, I think so. There are times I wonder about all the experiences I missed and what I might be doing now instead. Would I have some high-flying career or be living somewhere more exciting than here? Is Tom's life what I want, really? Once he'd gone and left Mum heartbroken, I did feel some pressure to stay local. I couldn't put Mum through that twice. But I also like living here. I've never had a huge desire to get away farther than the hour-long drive I have done.

Sometimes I feel embarrassed around new people, especially Jonathan's teacher friends (who clearly value education highly) and worry they might find out I don't have a degree and think I'm stupid. But even if I could go to university now, even if I was offered a place for free, I still don't know what I'd study. I have no dream career I'm working toward. It would be a waste of money, just going for the parties and the pride of having a degree, not in any real pursuit of knowledge or to follow my dreams. Maybe one day I'll find my calling, though.

I'm just glad Jonathan didn't fall in love with Up North and was happy to come closer to home to buy our little house and settle here with me—close enough to our parents to feel supported, but at enough of a distance from them that we felt like our independent lives were properly starting. Not going to university definitely helped us make this step earlier, as

I'd been able to work and save for three years straight. But even with a loan from Jonathan's parents, we were still only able to buy under the government's Help to Buy scheme, and that meant a new build. No matter how much DIY Jonathan does, it's impossible to make it feel properly homely. I want it to be like his parents' higgledy-piggledy house, all secret corners, spiderwebs and mice, an overgrown garden, and endless character and charm throughout. The kind of house you can imagine having a real adventure in, finding fairies in the garden or entire worlds in the backs of wardrobes.

When Amy decided to come back from Sheffield too after her job and boyfriend didn't work out, it was even better—both my favourite people were close to me again.

Chapter 31

"I've been sending Patrick more naked photos," I tell Lucy on our run a couple of days later. "It's kind of nerve-racking. Obviously it's my body, but also he's a photographer so I worry what he'll think of my photography skills. But that's been making me get creative with them, so it's fun. It's becoming a bit of a hobby."

"I don't know how you do it. I'm not sure I'd want to see how those pictures came out for me, let alone share them with anyone else!"

"You should try. It's made me see myself so differently. I'm loads more confident about my body now. You have to be a bit clever with the angles and lighting, but it's worth it."

He gives me little challenges to do sometimes too. Sometimes he'll suggest I do something in bed with Jonathan, just so I can tell him all about it afterwards. It makes sex with Jonathan much more exciting and I get to relive it all too, so it's double the fun. Last week he challenged me to wear a skirt with no underwear. All day I was aware of it, worried someone would notice and say something. I could feel the air around me, every gust of wind sending me into a minor panic. But at the end of the day, I got home and hopped on a video call with him, pulling up my skirt to reveal my nakedness underneath. He loved it!

"It does all sound exciting. Maybe a bit stressful too, though. I just don't know how you have time to fit it all in," Lucy tells me a little patronisingly. But then she pauses and looks a little more thoughtful. "I suppose it would be fun to be with someone new again. It's been a long time. I just think I'd be so scared; I'm not sure I'm brave enough for a first date anymore. And I don't think I could handle the thought of Dave being with someone else, so I wouldn't dare to even bring it up. He'd probably love the idea of finally having sex again, though, and I'd never see him again!"

Later than evening, Lucy texts and asks if she can see some of my pictures. I feel a rush as I choose a couple of my favourites to send to her. One is my ass in a tiny pair of denim shorts, pulled up as high as they'd go. I had to get into a really uncomfortable position, twisting my arm at an unnatural angle to get high enough to fit my whole ass into the picture. It was worth it though, I know I look great, and Jonathan and Patrick both confirmed that too. The other is my hand reaching into my pants. I'm lying down so my stomach seems flatter than I thought possible, making it my absolute favourite photo of myself ever.

Her response is incredible—she loves them, and she makes me feel beautiful and sexy and appreciated. Later on, Lucy sends me a picture of her own. She's put on lingerie that's sat at the back of her underwear drawer for years, never worn. Hot-pink lace underwear is the gorgeous contrast to her dark skin, high heels elongating her flawless legs even further, pink lipstick the perfect match to her underwear.

You look incredible! Like a stripper, in the best possible way.

I feel pretty amazing too! Freshly confident, she gives Dave the surprise of his life when she goes downstairs after putting the girls to bed.

It goes on to become an almost weekly ritual, sending each other sexy photos. The buzz we get from sharing these is indescribable and confidence-boosting in a way that sending them to Patrick isn't. She always replies immediately and appreciatively, whereas Patrick can take hours to reply, leaving me worried he doesn't like them or that I've gone too far. And with Patrick, I worry I'm only sending him my best angles, raising his expectations for when we meet again.

That doesn't matter with Lucy—she knows the real me.

Chapter 32

D ave and the girls go to visit his parents for the Easter weekend, so Lucy and I take the opportunity to go shopping. The sun is starting to fight its way through the clouds with glimpses of the summer to come, so we're scouring the shops for the perfect summer dress, trying on four or five at a time. We cram into the Topshop dressing room to help each other with zips and buttons, laughing as we twirl around in our colourful dresses, frayed denim short-shorts, and knitwear leftovers from the sale rail. I haven't had this much fun in ages.

We've both seen pictures of each other in our underwear plenty over the last few weeks, but I find myself averting my eyes as we get changed, a little shy. Somehow it feels different without the screens between us, without the opportunity to curate the image to be exactly how we want it. This is more real, unedited, imperfect, intimate, and it feels a little intrusive and uncomfortable to look at her freely. But that also makes it all the more alluring and intriguing when I catch a glimpse of her bare skin, a little bit naughty in its way.

At lunch, we make our way through two bottles of prosecco and don't manage to finish our shared goat's cheese and caramelised red onion pizza, even though it's my favourite. Giggling, we go to Tesco on our way back home and buy a couple more bottles and head back to Lucy's house to carry on.

At Lucy's, we pop open the bottles, put on music and our new dresses, dancing around her kitchen laughing. We realise all at once that we're starving and she raids the kitchen cupboards to pull together a feast of crisps and hummus, Bird's Eye potato waffles cooked in the toaster, her kids' lunch-box-sized chocolate bars. Sprawled out on the sofa feeling drunk and full, licking crisp salt off our fingers, we snuggle up warm and cosy together under a blanket and watch old episodes of *Friends* whilst I tell her all about my date with Patrick.

"I just blurted out *I want to kiss you* and I thought he'd do it straight away, but he just held my hand for an agonising moment first before giving me the most magical kiss."

Lucy's eyes meet mine from beneath her lashes.

"I want to kiss you," she mumbles, looking right at me and then quickly down at the table, a little embarrassed.

I'm taken aback. I wasn't expecting this at all and I'm not sure if it was just a drunk throwaway comment or a real request. I need time to digest what she said. I'm not used to her being vulnerable like this; she's always so confident. I'm doing what Patrick did and I know how long this moment must seem to her, but it's definitely not a game—I'm thinking. Does she mean it or is she just playing, or is she drunk and going to regret saying this in the morning? Do I want to? I haven't thought about this ever. I'm straight. I love men and everything about them. The weight and smell of a man looming over me, the rough, scratchy stubble as we kiss.

I love Lucy too. Spending time with her always makes me so

happy. She's gorgeous. If she were male, I'd definitely have given this proper thought before now and would most likely have gone straight in for the kiss, would probably have been doing everything I could to engineer this situation myself.

She looks up at me, big eyes through long feathery lashes, and I give her a little nod. I lean forward, kissing her tentatively. The kiss is soft and gentle, as warm and soothing as stroking a purring cat, a comfortable feeling. Our foreheads touch, hair hanging down and creating a private bubble around us, the world around us, Dave and Jonathan, forgotten. We pause and have a little giggle, releasing the nervous tension from the air.

My eyes meet hers, checking that this is okay. We both smile at each other, confirming that it is, and with that, we're kissing more deeply. I undo the back of the dress I zipped her into earlier and pull it over her head. I know she is uncomfortable about her body since having the girls, so I pull my own dress off too, trying to make things even. Our hands start to explore each other's bodies, her skin as dark as mine is pale.

I've never touched a woman like this before, but it feels good, natural, easy. I play with her small, dark nipples and neat little boobs, a few tiny stretch marks decorating them. I've never touched someone else's boob before; it's so soft. I kiss my way slowly down her body, trail my fingers along her C-section scar as I get closer to my destination. My body is alive with pleasure, every touch electric. The air feels charged with anticipation, as though time has stopped everywhere but here.

I've never done this before; I'm terrified I'll get it wrong, but I decide to just dive in before I can overthink it and talk myself out of it. I pull her white lacy pants slowly down, wondering if she wears these every day or if maybe she planned and hoped for this moment. The idea of her putting them on this morning, thinking she might be showing them to me later, is exciting.

I lick her like an ice cream, noticing how good she tastes, my tongue moving around every bit of her as I look into her eyes, trying to replicate some of what Ben did to me. I kiss and lick and suck, my fingers starting to explore her too. She's making noises that let me know I'm not so bad at this, despite my inexperience, her every moan and whimper setting me on fire.

I take a second to catch my breath, suddenly realising how drunk I am, my eyes warm. I start to wonder if this a terrible idea that we're both going to regret, but then we smile at each other, and the slight hint of nervousness behind her smile is so sweet and vulnerable, it makes me smile even wider before I go in for more.

I find and tease her clit with my tongue, and she lets out a satisfied sigh. I think back to high school talk and decide to try writing the alphabet with my tongue, a task that's more difficult and requires more concentration than I expected. I'm sure sex isn't supposed to involve so much thinking. I give up on the alphabet and try to use my whole tongue, my whole mouth, which seems to do the trick.

I've never given a moment's thought to doing this before with anyone. I try to liken the taste to something familiar but can't; it just tastes of sex, nothing else. It smells warm and clean and even a little earthy. I'm enjoying it more than I thought I would, and I don't want to stop.

I slip a finger inside her, soft and wet and warm, and try to move it with a similar rhythm to my tongue. Hooking my fingers around slightly, I find the ridged area I can't reach in myself very easily, and stroke there. I move my other hand to her hard nipple and soft breast. She's moaning away happily

138

now, so I must be getting something right. Hearing the sounds she's making is driving me crazy. I like feeling so powerful over this strong woman. I get faster and faster until she lets out a long loud moan and pulls me up to kiss her.

As we kiss, we wrap our legs around each other and my soaking-wet pussy finds the friction of her leg and rides away there. I can't believe how good, how right, it feels; I'm so close to orgasm already. She grabs my tits and sucks hard on my right nipple as I ride her leg to completion, falling down into her arms.

Fuck, I wasn't expecting that!

We quietly doze off together in each other's arms on the sofa, the wine sending us quickly into a deep sleep.

I wake up cold, confused, and uncomfortable with the bright light shining in my eyes.

Lucy is stirring next to me too and starts to get herself up off the sofa. "I'm going to go up to bed. Do you want to come?"

Leaving behind ketchup-smeared plates, dirty glasses, and our crumpled clothes, I follow her upstairs. She disappears off into the bathroom as I make myself comfortable in her lovely big bed. When she returns, it takes me a second too long to process what I'm seeing, and she notices and starts to make embarrassed noises and explanations, her arms uncomfortable as they try to find somewhere to settle on her body.

"God, I'm so sorry," I say. "What am I like? I literally had no idea you wore a wig—that was a bit of a surprise! You look beautiful, really beautiful," I assure her.

She does. Her hair is shorn to make room for her wig, leaving only tiny coils of hair decorating her scalp. Her smooth, blemish-free skin and features showed off in all their glory. I dread to think what I'd look like without my hair.

139

She's rubbing sweet-smelling oil into her hair, then wrapping it in a bright red silk scarf as she explains, "It's just easier than trying to tame my hair. I had to do it when I was working as a solicitor, or I wouldn't have been taken seriously, especially being so young then. I just got used to it and never stopped. That bob feels like part of me now." She leans in closer with a cheeky grin and stage-whispers, "Also, it really pisses my mum off that I don't wear my natural hair, and that's a little bit irresistible!"

"You're gorgeous either way," I tell her, snuggling in to fall asleep.

Throughout the night, we seem to always be touching each other somehow—she's spooned up against me, or just our fingers touching when we get too hot. Every time I move, I'm terrified I'll wake her and ruin her night of child-free sleep, but she seems to sleep deeply all night, letting out an occasional tiny snore. When Jonathan snores, it drives me crazy. I'm always having to roll him over to try and get him to stop snoring. But every snore and sound from Lucy makes me smile.

Chapter 33

I wake with a pounding headache early in the morning and watch Lucy sleeping peacefully, an occasionally tiny and adorable snore escaping her beautiful, full lips. Her skin is smooth and flawless, but now I'm closer to her than ever before, I notice the smattering of freckles across her nose, a tiny scar by her right eye. I sneak off to the toilet, sticking my head under the tap to guzzle as much water as I can before splashing my face and wiping yesterday's mascara from under my eyes with a tissue.

I climb back into bed and snuggle into her, kissing the back of her neck and behind her ear as she starts to stir. I lose my nerve for a moment and worry she doesn't want this now that she's sober, but then she kisses me back and keeps on kissing me. With her hand gently stroking my back, we grind against each other's legs. I make my way down her body and start to lick her again, two fingers inside her. I get her close but don't think I quite push her over the edge. I desperately want to make her come but I remind myself it's okay if it doesn't happen. I've had sex enough times and not come but still had a great time.

She starts to move, pulling me up to kiss her. We both kneel on the bed as she puts her fingers inside me. She's grinding against my leg now; I can feel how wet she is. We keep kissing, kneeling there, touching each other all over, moaning into each other's ears and mouths.

She gently pushes me back so I'm lying on the bed and then she's licking me, sucking, kissing, her tongue flicking over my clit. She's making hungry noises that are driving me wild. Her fingers enter me and hit just the right spot, making me come. I'm shaking, my breathing heavy, but she doesn't stop. She keeps going, keeps touching and licking until I come again and again until I can take no more.

She lies next to me, our sweaty faces close to each other on the shared pillow, and we doze off again.

When we wake a little later, my headache seems to have lifted, and a strong wave of guilt and fear floods through my body. Was that cheating? I need to see Jonathan, now. I think he's okay with me being with a woman—it doesn't bother him in the same way that me being with a man does. Our whole thing was meant to be about having the freedom to take opportunities that come our way. So, no, I don't think I was cheating on Jonathan. But Lucy? She was definitely cheating on Dave, and I let her.

"I need to get back home to Jonathan," I say, giving her a kiss on her cheek and quietly getting myself dressed and ready to go.

It surprises me how much this urgency to see Jonathan and reconnect with him takes over me every time I'm with someone else. However much fun I'm having, being sure Jonathan is okay is my priority and overrides any other desires I may have.

"I slept with Lucy last night," I tell Jonathan straight away when I get home.

"I know."

"I mean, we had sex."

He goes quiet, his face unreadable.

"That's okay, isn't it?"

"I'm not sure yet. I wasn't expecting that. I just need some time to process it."

As he walks away, I realise I need to process this too. I hadn't ever seriously considered doing anything with a girl, unless perhaps in a threesome situation with Jonathan there too. I didn't think I was interested at all. I'm still not sure I am. I don't feel ready to suddenly start calling myself bisexual. This was about Lucy specifically, not girls in general. I think.

I've got no idea how Lucy is feeling, how long she might've been preparing for that moment or if it was just a drunk, spontaneous thing she's now regretting. Or maybe she's wondering if I'm regretting it? I text her to try to settle any concerns she might be having about that: *I had fun last night. Sorry I had to leave so early x*

I know her husband won't like it. She never has sex with him, but she'll cheat on him and do it with someone else? That's not going to go down well, is it? What have I done? Have I just jeopardised her entire marriage and her family, on a drunken whim? I can't believe I've done this, and so soon after telling Amy what a bastard Matt is for cheating on his wife—and on her too, I suppose.

Or maybe I'm wrong and he will like it. Maybe it'll really turn him on and give their sex life the boost it needs. And where would that leave me? They'll suddenly sort out all their problems and start having sex again and be happy, and she won't need me anymore. I'm not sure yet what I want from Lucy, but I do know that whatever happens, I don't want to lose her friendship.

I find myself stroking the scrunchie she gave me, its softness comforting—a connection to her.

I make Jonathan a coffee and follow him into the lounge. I sit at the other end of the sofa from him, the sofa feeling bigger than ever, a divide I'm desperate to cross, but I can sense he's not ready for that yet.

"I just wish you'd told me before so I could've prepared for it."

"But I didn't know. There was nothing to tell you before! I wasn't planning on doing it or even hoping to. It was as much a surprise to me as it is to you."

He breathes hard out of both nostrils. "Why do you have to be so impatient? Couldn't you have waited and spoken to me first? This might have been okay if I'd just had some time to think about it."

"We just got lost in the moment—you know what it's like. I didn't want to break the spell. I really thought this would be alright. It's what we always said, wasn't it, about taking opportunities that come our way?"

"She's your friend. I don't know how I feel about you being with someone I know. I don't know how to deal with it. It feels so public. I can't just ignore it and pretend it's not really happening when it's someone I know too."

I sort of understand what he's saying, but I wish he could stop wanting to ignore it and pretend it's not happening. I'd give anything to be one step closer to him welcoming and embracing this as something that benefits him, and us, not just me. "Isn't it better that it's someone you know and like and trust? And I can go out with her and not have to worry about being seen and having people ask awkward questions. It would be so much easier."

"When did you decide you were a lesbian anyway? You never mentioned this before."

"Oh, come on, I had sex one time with a friend who happens to be female, that's all."

"And what does her husband think of all this?"

He's got me there. A fresh wave of guilt washes over me. It's not just Dave, it's her girls too, Hannah and Freya. If I'm the catalyst to their family being torn apart, how will I live with myself? Jonathan is right—once the moment had started, we should've put a stop to it and taken some time to think about it first. If it was meant to be, we both could've waited a little longer, couldn't we?

He shakes his head with a snort as he realises why I'm taking so long to answer. "He doesn't know, does he? I thought this was supposed to be all about being open and honest with everyone all the time. So, what do you want now? First Ben, then Patrick, now Lucy. When does it end? When will you be done with this so we can go back to normal?"

I don't have an answer to that. I definitely want to see Patrick again and I definitely want to have sex with him. I definitely want to keep seeing Lucy, and I loved having sex with her, but I don't know if it was a one-off or the start of something. And if I'm spending time with her anyway, does it really matter what we're doing in that time? Can't we just see what happens? I hate that the decision doesn't feel like mine and Lucy's, but Jonathan's and Dave's.

It matters first what they think about it before we can even take our own feelings and desires into account. As much as I want to respect their feelings and not hurt anyone, it just doesn't feel fair.

Chapter 34

Memories of Lucy are still fresh in my mind when she comes into the café a few days later. I'm sitting with Frank as he tells me about how he and Ethel met, back when they were my age. A real story of courtship—and plenty of patience by the sounds of it.

Lucy's looking lovely, wearing a little too much makeup, and I realise with a flutter that she's nervous to see me. No-one's ever dressed up like that for me before; it feels good! Julie serves her, and she takes a seat, keeps glancing over at me. I want to join her, so I give her a big smile to show her this as I listen to the rest of Frank's tale.

"We met right at the end of the war at a dance in Dorset. You loved those dances, didn't you, dear? She was always in a different dress every week, swapping them with her friends. She'd draw stocking lines up the back of her legs, I've got no idea how she got them so straight, but she always did."

"You've still kept your fashion sense, haven't you!"

And she has. I don't think I've ever seen in her exactly the same outfit twice. She's always got gorgeous brooches and other accessories to finish off her outfit, clearly takes a pride in her appearance. She smiles back at me but doesn't say a word.

"Ethel liked the city, really. She didn't know how to be in the country, but I helped her learn to love the outdoors. We used to go out spotting all the lovely birds and we still love watching them together now, don't we, dear?"

"That's so lovely. You obviously still love each other very much even after all these years. It gives us all hope, I think!"

I notice Julie is shaking chocolate powder over Lucy's cappuccino, so I make my excuses to get back to work. I get to the till just in time so I can offer to take Lucy's drink over to her.

As I place the drink in front of her, she tells me quietly, "I'm not going to tell him."

With that, my decision is made. "Then it can't happen again."

I walk away slowly, my bottom lip trembling a little as I realise how much I really do want it to happen again. But one drunken cheating incident can be explained away and forgiven. If it happens again, it becomes something different, something I don't want to be a part of.

That evening, Jonathan is out with Sarah for a sunset bike ride, so I call Patrick.

"I need to tell you something. I had sex with my friend—is that okay with you?"

"Of course it is! The more, the merrier. I just want us all to have fun!"

"She's married, though, and she isn't going to tell her husband. So basically, it was cheating, wasn't it? I feel really bad about it."

"Oh. Well, you and Jonathan have an agreement. If she did it with you without something like that in place, then that's on her, not you. You can't go back on it now, so don't waste your energy feeling guilty."

I'm not sure I entirely agree with this logic, but I feel my shoulders falling a little, some of my guilt lifted.

"Anyway, so you did it with a girl? I didn't know you were into that! Will you tell me what happened?"

I go on to tell him what happened with Lucy. This gives me the effect I was hoping for but didn't get from Jonathan. To say he's turned on barely covers it. He wants to hear every juicy detail, and I'm enjoying telling him about it.

"I can't wait to see you again and feel your hands on me at last," I tell him.

"Me neither. But it's difficult at the moment. Kate's mum has got worse; I need to be here with the kids."

I'll have to take a leaf out of Frank's book and be more patient.

As I come away from the call, I realise just how much I enjoyed being with Lucy, and how much I want to do it again. I punch my pillow in frustration, at myself for saying we couldn't do it again and at Jonathan and Dave for making it that way. I'm frustrated not to be able to see Patrick too, but knowing he wants to, and that Jonathan is okay with it, is enough for now.

Chapter 35

"Who are you? Leave me alone! I don't know you! Help!"

Ethel is shouting in the café. Frank is by her side, trying to help her with her coat like he always does, but today she's having none of it. She's surprisingly strong for such a frail-looking lady, elbows poking out fiercely in every direction. Frank's usually cheery face is grey and pale today, sad and exhausted.

"Here, let me help."

Ethel allows me to help her with her coat, and I offer to walk them home whilst Julie holds the fort at the café.

Ethel chats away happily enough with me, but flat-out ignores Frank the whole walk home. "Sorry, dear, I'm all muddled. I didn't sleep very well last night; those blasted trains were keeping me up."

I'm confused, they don't live anywhere near a train station. I look to Frank, who explains, "She gets mixed up sometimes. She grew up right next to a train station and sometimes she finds herself there in her head."

I'm not entirely sure what's going on, I just know I can see his heart breaking right in front of my eyes. We walk slowly back to their pretty little cottage, honeysuckle around the doorway like something straight out of Beatrix Potter. I follow them in and help Ethel get settled with a cup of tea in front of *The Chase* on the TV.

Frank beckons me into the bright kitchen. I hadn't registered it in the café, but he's lost weight; he seems even smaller than usual. We sit quietly for a minute or two and I notice tears forming in his eyes. "I can't cope anymore."

He tells me about Ethel's dementia. First it wasn't being able to work out money, or forgetting simple words. She was understandably frustrated all the time and had lashed out at him more than once. Then the nightmares started; she'd wake up screaming. Now they're sleeping in separate rooms.

"We've slept side-by-side for over fifty years. I can't bear it; I can't bear it not having her there next to me. I'm so angry. It's so unfair. I wish it could be me rather than her—she doesn't deserve this."

I don't know what to say. I just want to cuddle him—them—up and try to make it all better, but I don't know how to do that. I may not know much about Dementia, but I do know it's going to get worse and not better.

Frank goes on to tell me more. Searching her brain for answers to simple questions wasn't working anymore, so Ethel started physically looking for them, leaving open drawers and cupboards in her wake wherever she went. She started accusing Frank of moving or stealing things, but when Frank denied it, she became paranoid someone was breaking into the house and taking things.

"The house is a mess. She can't do all the things she used to do to keep it nice, and I don't know what I'm doing. I'm letting her down. She shouldn't have to live like this."

Even within their own home, this beautiful home which they've shared for more than half a century and raised their sons in, she can't find her way around anymore. Can't find the bedroom or the toilet by herself. She follows him around all day like a lost sheep. The hand-holding I admired in them wasn't just out of love now; he was scared of losing her if he didn't hold on to her.

Recently she's started to forget the people in her life. Her eldest son, Andy, has to introduce himself every time he comes around, which is becoming even less frequent, and her youngest son lives too far away for her to remember at all anymore.

Up until now, he's coped, picked up the slack, managing to hide most of it, so they've been able to carry on almost as normal—I certainly wasn't aware of how serious this was. If I'm really honest, I feel bad I hardly even noticed there was a problem at all, beyond a little confusion.

But today, today, she didn't recognise her own husband. Worse, she feared him. The man who's been by her side for over fifty years, loving her so fiercely, is no longer a source of happiness and support to her.

Listening to him is heart-breaking. I've been watching them, admiring them, for months. I've never seen a couple so devoted to each other, so happy in each other's company. I can't imagine how this has happened. It's so unfair.

"Our boys have been saying it for weeks now. She's going to have to go into a care home, isn't she?"

As I walk along the busy street back to the café, I'm lost in thought, wondering how my life will turn out. Whether I'll have to make this heart-wrenching decision about Jonathan or

151

my parents one day, or if someone will have to make it about me. Who would that be if I never have children? Will I have a whole team of people who love me in all different ways, who'll be there to look after me and each other, or will I have pushed everyone away by wanting too much and not being satisfied with what I've got?

I like the idea of it being a team effort, everyone supporting each other and the burden not all falling on one person. Poor Frank is trying to care for Ethel whilst also trying to deal with his own grief, as the woman he's loved for so many years is disappearing before his eyes.

I want to talk to Lucy, to tell her about Ethel, but I know I can't. I need to put some distance between us whilst we both sort our heads out.

Chapter 36

"She's here! Do you want to come out and meet her?"

Bright and early on Saturday morning, Sarah's car pulls up outside our house to take Jonathan away for the bike race weekend. Jonathan rushes out like an excited puppy greeting its owner. I do want to meet her; I'm dying to meet her, in fact—especially since my realisation about how good it would be to have a whole team of us loving and looking after each other. But right now, it's very early, and my head is in a bit of a spin at the prospect. He's never mentioned meeting her before, so why today?

What if she doesn't like me and tells Jonathan to leave me? What if I don't like her and become uncomfortable with them seeing each other? What if I go out and say hello and see what happens? It's going to happen sooner or later, so why not at six a.m. in my pyjamas? She is just a friend, after all. I don't know what I'm getting in such a fuss about.

"Okay, give me a minute to sort myself out I bit first," I shout down to him, tugging a hairbrush through my tangled hair and a toothbrush over my teeth, then pulling on a jumper in an attempt to look at least a bit more presentable.

Outside, Sarah is somehow absolutely stunning in full Lycra, even with her dark hair slicked down ready for a bike helmet. When he told me he didn't fancy her, I just assumed she wasn't all that. But she is. All. That. And here I am, fresh out of bed, toothpaste down my jumper, fluffy bunny slippers on my feet. In contrast, used to being up and about at this stupid time, Sarah is a big ball of bouncy energy.

"Hi! You must be Sophie! It's so good to meet you at last. Jon has told me so much about you, I feel like I know you already!"

"Nice to meet you. Same, he talks about you a lot." *But he never mentioned that you were American,* I add in my head, confused as to why he'd leave out a detail like that. What else isn't he telling me?

I'm awkward, blushing like a schoolgirl, pulling at my jumper nervously. I can hardly look her in the eye. What's wrong with me?

Jonathan has finished putting his bike on the roof rack and comes bouncing over to me, a huge grin on his face as he gives me a quick kiss and goes to get into the car. "All set, let's go! See you tomorrow evening, Soph!"

Soph? He never calls me Soph.

And with that, they're gone, leaving me shellshocked in the street in my slippers.

What was that?

Sarah is gorgeous, stunning. Do I fancy her more than he does? Have I opened up some bisexual part of my brain that was closed before? Or am I just desperate for her to like me, because I'm scared she'll tell Jonathan to leave me if she doesn't think I'm worthy of him?

Sarah and Jonathan get on so well—they seem to love spending time together, can't get enough of it. They have my full blessing, so why is nothing happening there? Is he lying to me? Are they going to go away and finally realise they're perfect for each other and I'm going to lose him and be all alone, and it'll be all my own fault for starting this?

After a couple more hours back in bed, I calm myself down and spend Saturday enjoying being by myself, just lazing around, wondering if this is what life would be like if Jonathan did come back and tell me he's leaving me for Sarah. Or that he's thought it all through more and it's all too much and he's leaving me to be on his own. Maybe it wouldn't be so bad; I'm enjoying the quiet at least, leaving the washing up until I want to do it rather than feeling pressured to do it the moment I finish eating.

It helps me realise I'm not scared to break up. If anything, I'm almost excited at the prospect of living alone for the first time in my life, and that helps me understand that I do really want Jonathan. I choose to be with him; there's no fear holding us together, only desire. I will fight for us to stay together, but not at any cost. I won't give up on everything I want just because that would be easier. And even if I said I'd give it up, now that he knows how much I want it, how could he ever really trust me?

I'm annoyed that Patrick wasn't able to see me this weekend when I have so much time to myself, but I don't feel like I can say this to anyone, least of all Patrick, who's taken his kids on a camping trip far from any phone signal, whilst Kate is staying at her mum's for the weekend to give her dad a break.

I decide to call Amy to talk to her about Lucy, Sarah, and my sexuality. I've got no idea what she'll make of it all, whether she might even be jealous that I didn't do my experimenting with her. Part of me almost wishes Amy and Lucy had done it instead of me so I could still see Lucy and not have all this guilt and confusion driving me crazy.

Amy answers the phone in tears, and I know this isn't the time for my troubles. She needs me more than I need her right now. "I didn't want to tell you; I know it was stupid. I carried on seeing Matt."

"Oh, Amy."

There's a pause in which I can hear her trying to calm herself down, to stop crying so she can tell me more. I want to reach through my phone and hold her. "His wife found out again—of course she did—and now he's chosen her and said he never wants to speak to me again."

"When did all this happen?"

"Last week. I got a horrible message from her, and then he called me to say he was blocking my number. I'm at my mum's now. She doesn't know the details, just that I've had a breakup. But she's annoyed that she never met the guy, says it can't have been that serious if I never told her about him or introduced her to him."

"That's not fair. I'm so sorry. Let me know when you're back."

"Will do. Love you."

"Love you too."

By Sunday, I'm bored stiff. I would normally have gone out for a run with Lucy today, but I can't motivate myself to go out alone.

I think of poor Frank and Ethel, the decision they have to face now, the guilt and loneliness he'll feel if she goes into a care home. If I miss Jonathan this much after one night, I can't begin to imagine how much Frank will miss Ethel. I resolve to be there to support him however I can, to start popping in at least once a week.

Needing a little boost after meeting Sarah, being away from Jonathan, and not being able to contact Patrick or Lucy, I impulsively message Ellis, the first guy from the dating app I chatted with. He seems pleased to hear from me and we exchange a few chatty messages before he asks me if I'd like to hop on a video chat again. There's nothing stopping me from doing it, and surely this is what I was hoping for when I messaged him? But I realise I don't have any intention of meeting him, that I've just used him because I'm lonely and feeling sorry for myself. Whilst he looks hot and seems keen, I don't get the same rush of excitement from his messages that I did with Ben, or that I still do with Patrick, so I decide it's not worth putting Jonathan through it. I say no to the call and bring the conversation to a close before deleting his number.

Instead, I'll play alone. Too often I rush this and try to hide it for Jonathan's sake, but he's not here today, so I'm going to take my time. I put music on and choose a couple of toys to play with.

I stroke my skin gently, my boobs, my stomach, my hips. I turn my vibrator on and play with it over my pants, teasing myself, grazing my nipple with my thumb.

Just as I'm starting to get into it, I hear a knock next door. I imagine it's my door, a delivery driver. I have to rush to answer the door, and he can't help but notice my flushed, breathless state. I imagine him being embarrassed, blushing, looking away as he notices I haven't covered myself up properly.

Do you need any help? he'll ask, gaining confidence and stepping into the house.

I imagine him pushing me up against the closed door, unable to make it any further before he has to touch me. His lips on my nipples whilst he removes his cock from his trousers and fucks me standing against the door, my legs up around his waist, the letterbox clattering as we slam against the door.

Shit! That didn't take long! My whole body is shaking as I come hard. My vibrator is still buzzing away inside me. I want to take it out, it's too much now, but I can't quite muster the energy to do it, so there it stays for a little longer.

I lie there, wrapped up in the duvet and my own inner glow, and fall asleep.

Soon I wake up feeling refreshed and calm and take the opportunity to give my toys a thorough bath, washing and drying them lovingly and putting them all on to charge. Too often I feel the need to hide the fact that I use them, and rush cleaning them or don't charge them fully, but now I have time to do it right. This is a reminder of how much I enjoy being alone, having some time to myself to do whatever I want in peace. Between work and Jonathan and going out, I'm very rarely at home by myself and I'm surprised how much I've enjoyed this time alone.

Returning from his trip later on, Jonathan is like a new person: energised and proud of completing the race. He shows me his medal, giving me a blow-by-blow account of every twist and turn he faced. Seeing him like this is sexy; he seems taller, fitter, funnier even. His excitement is infectious, and I can't help but wonder if something happened between him and Sarah when they were away. He assures me it didn't, but I don't believe him, and I can't let it go.

"Why don't you just tell me? I don't mind, I'd be happy for you. Just don't lie to me!"

He stares at me in disbelief, his arms outstretched pleadingly as he tries to answer my unfounded accusations. "What the hell? Nothing happened and, even if it did, I know you'd be okay with it, so why would I lie about it? You're being insane. I don't need this." He storms off, angry and disappointed.

I don't know why this is bothering me so much. Maybe I just really wanted them to have sex to even the playing field a little, assuage some of my guilt.

Eventually I realise what's really going on. I'm jealous. I'm jealous he's found someone and connected so much with her that sex is utterly unimportant, they've got something deeper than that. I'm jealous he gets to spend so much time with her, whilst I've only met Patrick once and can't really see Lucy at all at the moment. I'm jealous that his relationship with her is socially acceptable and he doesn't have to worry about being seen in public when he's with her. I wonder if I'm jealous of her specifically; maybe I really do fancy her? If I do, what does that mean? For me, me and Jonathan, me and Patrick, me and Lucy?

I take a minute to let this all sink in properly before following him into the lounge. "I'm really sorry. I think I'm feeling jealous that you get to spend so much time with Sarah and I haven't quite managed to find someone like that yet. It's not your fault. You've done so well; I'm proud of you!"

I straddle him on the sofa, kissing him hard as I pull his cock out and play with it, a cheeky grin on my face. I raise my eyebrow to enquire whether he's forgiven my stupid and inappropriate reaction, to which he nods. Looking into his eyes, I move my pants to the side under my skirt and slide onto his cock. He tugs on my ponytail gently, and I arch my back, thrusting my nipple into his mouth. He buries his head into my chest as I ride him until he comes.

Chapter 37

At Mum's birthday course, as we whisk egg whites for our macarons, Mum and I are getting on better than we have in a long time. She seems lighter than normal, perhaps because here we're equals; there's less of a battle than we usually have in her house, where she simultaneously tries to mother me and wants to see me being a grownup.

"This takes me back! Do you remember how much you used to love helping me in the kitchen? You were always coming up with menus and playing café!"

Even though I was only small, I do remember loving our time together in the kitchen. We used to do cooking any time it was just me and Mum at home, and I loved to help her make everyone's birthday cakes. For Tom's tenth birthday, I spent hours poking chocolate buttons into his hedgehog cake, wanting to get them just right for him. He loved that cake.

"We did have good times, didn't we?" she continued. "I know it wasn't always easy, but I was doing my best."

Once, when Mum was late home from work and the grumpy teenage Tom was holed away in his room, I remember deciding to cook dinner myself. It was just pasta and I think I managed to do a pretty okay job of it, apart from overcooking it a bit. But in the process, I managed to spill oil down the front of my only school pinafore. When Mum got home, instead of being proud of me for sorting out dinner, she was angry at me for ruining my uniform. I don't know what she did to sort it out, but by the next morning she'd rustled up a new skirt from somewhere. As much as I wish she could've been around more for us when I was little, she did work so hard to try to give me and Tom the best she could, and I'm grateful.

"I know you were, Mum. I've turned out all right, haven't I? So you can't have done too badly!"

Nervously, we hold our bowls of whisked egg whites over our heads to check if they're ready before adding our sugar, almond flour, and choosing our flavours and colours. Pistachio and raspberry for me, chocolate and lemon for Mum. We pipe them out, bang out the air bubbles, and leave them to set a little before putting them in the oven.

We watch them cooking slowly, waiting for exactly the right moment to take them out of the oven and leave them to cool before we take a break. They seem to have turned out surprisingly well. Mum and I have a walk around the pretty gardens outside and sit on a bench beneath a weeping willow. It's idyllic.

When they're finally cooled, we pipe our fillings into them: pistachio buttercream, raspberry jam, chocolate ganache, lemon curd. They look incredible, all those pretty colours!

After such a good day together, I want to introduce Mum to Frank, and I'm sure he'd welcome visitors. Ethel has been in the care home for three days now, and he must be finding it lonely and hard to adjust to living alone.

Armed with a box of our pretty pastel-coloured macarons,

that evening I take Mum to Frank's house. He greets us both with a big smile as we make our way into his house. His old joyful self shines through with the smile, but he can't hide how tired and grey he's looking.

I go to the kitchen to make the tea. Frank has left a couple of letters out for me to check through like he always does. He can't bear to throw junk mail away, convinced he'll accidentally throw out something important, so he gets me to double check it before it can go in the bin.

When I come back, Frank is proudly showing Mum some of his watercolour paintings that are up on the walls, and Mum's asking questions about them—many of them are local landscapes she recognises, and each one has its own story. She glances over at me with a proud smile on her face, which hits me weirdly. Seeing her pride now is tinged with a sadness at how unusual this feeling is.

Frank points for me to sit in Ethel's usual chair, the chair with the best view of the garden. "Ethel always used to sit there. Seeing you in it now reminds me of when she was about your age and the boys were little. They'd sit at her feet, telling her all about their adventures whilst she knitted, wrapping the wool around their outstretched hands. You don't know how lucky you are to be young, your whole life ahead of you."

Frank goes quiet, lost in thoughts and memories.

We're all watching the birds in the garden, a robin on the bird feeder, when he mumbles, "I just can't believe she's gone. My Ethel. She was my everything. What am I going to do without her?"

There's nothing I can say, so I simply take his hand and hope it'll bring him some comfort. "Why don't we visit her together tomorrow?" I offer, and a tear rolls down his cheek as he nods in agreement.

"I'd like to come along too. She sounds like such a lovely lady. It would be an honour to meet her," says Mum importantly, smiling at Frank, who beams back at her.

"She'd like that a lot," he says.

After a while, Frank's conversation slows down, and I notice his eyes starting to droop a little, so Mum and I leave, promising to be back tomorrow to visit Ethel with him.

Mum and I return home and share a bottle of wine as she asks me about Frank and Ethel and how I got to know them. Jonathan is out watching the World Cup with some of the other teachers. Usually I visit Mum with Jonathan, and Dad is around too. It's rare to spend time just the two of us. I haven't felt this close to Mum in years; it's nice.

I find myself wanting to tell her about Patrick. I want to talk about Lucy too, but I'm still confused about exactly how I'm feeling, what I want, what's even possible, so I decide not to. One thing at a time.

I have no idea how she'll react, but I'm excited about Patrick and it feels like I'm lying to her, hiding an important part of myself—something that makes me happy—by not telling her about him.

I take a big, courage-building gulp of wine. "Mum, I need to tell you something."

I see a gleam of excitement appear in her eye, which I know I need to quash quickly.

"I'm not pregnant and we're not getting married, if that's what you're thinking. Jonathan and I are happy as we are. But I've met someone else, like a boyfriend, and Jonathan knows about it—it's not an affair." I garble it all out at once, wanting to get the whole story out before she can start to react. She's

163

keeping a very straight face, not giving anything away. My palms are sweating, my heart beating faster as I brace myself for her reaction. "He's called Patrick and he's married, and his wife knows too. We've only met once, but he's really lovely and he makes me happy. He's the cherry on my cake."

Mum is sitting very still, her face expressionless as she takes this in and tries to decide how she feels about it. Waiting for a response from her feels almost as scary as some of the conversations Jonathan and I have had about all this.

Her face erupts into what I hope is a genuine smile, her eyes twinkling. "Oh, sweetie, I knew something was going on. You seem different lately; you've blossomed. He's obviously doing you good, so I'm pleased for you. But I don't really want to know any more about it, if that's okay with you? Back in my day, we just got on with these things quietly. We didn't all have to talk about everything endlessly."

I'm not too sure what to make of that, but it feels good to have got it out in the open, not to have to worry she'll find out some other way from someone else and not understand what it is. Her disinterest hurts a little, though—how can she not want to know more? It could've been such a good opportunity to get a bit closer, and now it's gone. It's almost worse than her being angry or disappointed in me. I think back to Tom coming out—the tears from Mum, the shouting from Dad—and realise I'm being ridiculous. I'm lucky she's been so accepting.

Mum comes with Frank and I to visit Ethel in the care home in the morning. Between us, we scoff all of the remaining macarons, Ethel admiring the pretty colours but not saying a word for our whole visit. We sit in silence for much of the time, occasionally pointing out the nice things in Ethel's room: a bunch of flowers, a picture of their sons as babies, their wedding photograph.

After about half an hour, Ethel starts to get a bit agitated, and the carer suggests we leave so she can rest. Mum and I get up to go, but Frank wants to stay for longer; he's happy just to be there with her quietly while she sleeps.

Mum gives me a great big hug as we get to her car. I don't think she's hugged me like that since I was a kid.

"Mum, why didn't we see more of your parents growing up?" We've never talked about this. I have no idea what she's going to say, but now I've found how much I enjoy spending time with Frank and Ethel, it makes me wonder why I didn't have more time with my own grandparents.

"Oh, it was silly. My mum didn't like your dad; she didn't think he was good enough for me. Or maybe she did think he was enough for me, but she'd just hoped for better for her daughter and it was me who wasn't good enough. Whatever it was, really she'd just wanted me to escape the kind of life she'd had. When I met your dad and got pregnant so young, it was obvious that wasn't going to happen. There was a big fallout. Horrible things were said by us both and we never made up properly."

All this worrying I do about letting my parents down by not giving them grandchildren, and Mum let hers down by having them! I just can't believe anyone could continue with that kind of a grudge even once the baby came along, their own grandchild. "That's so sad. I'm sorry."

"I guess I understand her better now. I wanted the same for you two, and I'm so proud that you've both done it. You've broken the cycle, got out of the council estate, and now look at you. Both of you are living your lives on your own terms. Grandma would be proud. And so am I. Just don't lose sight of

165

how good Jonathan is. Don't throw him away for a bit of fun."

"That's not... I'm not," I start to explain, but she waves me off, satisfied she's made her point, and gets in her car to drive home.

Chapter 38

J ulie has been giving me funny looks all morning in the café. I don't know what's wrong with her, but then Jonathan appears at lunchtime with a wink, and I know something's going on. He whisks me away, having secretly arranged with Julie for me to have a couple of days off. We get in the car, even though I'm still in my work clothes with nothing packed and I have no idea where we're going.

"How did you wangle this? It's Saturday! What's Julie going to do?"

"Don't be silly. She can survive without you for a couple of days. You're not so indispensable, you know."

Indispensable or not, I can't believe Julie has agreed to this. It's always been a nightmare trying to get time off in summer.

"She's really pleased with you; she was telling me how hard you've been working lately and that you deserve a break."

When did she tell him that?

Soon we pull up to a farm in the middle of nowhere and he checks us into a cosy shepherd's hut. An enormous bed looks out over rolling hills, cosy armchairs are set in front of a log burner, and outside is a hot tub. I can't quite believe how lovely it is. I can feel my shoulders fall and my breathing slow as I relax into this new setting.

"How did you find this place?"

"Sarah helped me. It was her idea. I've packed you a bag too."

Good old Sarah! I should've known. He'd never have come up with something like this on his own. It would've taken hours of discussions trying to find the best deal, sucking all the fun out of booking a break. And then we'd have ended up somewhere awful just because the deal was too good to miss. But he hasn't scrimped here at all, as far as I can tell. It's lovely. Sarah might've encouraged him to book this and helped him find the right place, but he's still paid for it and sorted it all out with Julie. I squeeze his arm tight and snuggle into his shoulder as we quietly take in the view. I haven't felt this calm in a long time.

Warm bubbles rush pleasantly around us as we sit naked opposite each other in the hot tub, chatting aimlessly. Ducking down so my chin is resting on top of the water, I swim toward him and kiss him, grabbing his dick and gently playing with it until it's hard. I lower myself onto him and ride him gently, bubbles rushing around us as we take in the beautiful sunset, the sky impossibly pink and orange.

"I got the Head of Year promotion. I'm going to be the youngest Head of Year in the school," he whispers in my ear, voice filled with pride.

All those late nights spent tiredly planning and marking when I wanted him to pay me attention, the early mornings dashing into school when I wanted him to stay in bed with me, seem worth it now. I feel bad for moaning about them, but now his hard work has paid off. Of course I'm happy for him, but part of me is worried how much extra work this might mean for him and how that might affect our time together.

We spend the next forty-eight hours lazing around together, in and out of the hot tub, drinking hot chocolates as we watch the sun set, reading, talking, kissing, and having mind-blowing sex. Time stands still. There's nowhere to be, no DIY or housework to be done, nothing to rush around for.

It's just us. I feel closer to him than ever, perfectly content.

Chapter 39

Frank visits Ethel every day in the care home. It's been nearly two months, and she's settled in now, and can't remember living anywhere else. Although she isn't usually sure who Frank is, sometimes confusing him with her own father, she always seems pleased to see him and appears to feel safe with him now. They don't do anything. The laughter they've shared throughout their lives is gone. Their sons can hardly bear to visit; it's too hard seeing her like this, all the joy snuffed out of her, wrapped up in a blanket in a too-hot room with the TV blaring. She just sits there in a chair all day. Doesn't talk to anyone, doesn't go out in the garden, can't understand books or what's happening on the TV.

I try to visit with him every Monday on my day off. It feels a bit awkward—she's always friendly with me, but clearly has no idea who I am or why I've come to see her.

Seeing Frank alone in the café would've been heart-breaking, but Amy often pops in on her lunch break to have a cup of tea with him, and other customers sometimes invite him to join them too. He makes Amy laugh just as much as Ethel used to, and he's happy to share his slice of cake with her too.

Sometimes, if he comes in at the end of the day, I walk him

home and stay with him a while. He tells me stories from his life, how his visits with Ethel have been that week. But often we just sit quietly, watching and listening to the birds in his garden.

Frank reminds me often how short life is and not to waste it or live with regrets. This prompts me to get in touch with Lucy again, and I arrange to meet her for a drink soon. It's been nearly three months since I saw her last, and I miss her terribly. Next, I push Patrick to introduce me to Kate, something I've been thinking about for a long time. He sends me her number, leaving me to make the first move. I sit on it for an hour or two, wondering how on Earth to start this conversation.

Hi, I'm Sophie. It's nice to meet you, I text eventually.

Hi! You too! Pat's told me so much about you.

And that's it. We hit it off straight away. The relief is palpable, not just to know that she's genuinely okay with me, but to finally talk to someone who gets it. It's nice to hear something other than *I understand but I couldn't do it myself* like Lucy and Amy say. Instead, she tells me her own stories, making me feel normal and valid for wanting it at all.

Kate seems to relish the opportunity not to have to talk about her mum just as much as Patrick likes to talk about it with me, and I feel lucky to have found this special position in both of their lives.

Two days after Kate and I start chatting, Patrick finally suggests meeting again. I wonder how much control she may have had over the delay so far, but I'm glad that whatever I've said over the last couple of days seems to have reassured her.

After all that's happened with Lucy, I don't know how Jonathan is going to feel about this.

"Patrick has asked if I can see him next week for a day date."

Jonathan turns his head suddenly to look at me; he seems a little disorientated by this. "I didn't realise that was still going on. You haven't mentioned him for ages."

"You said you didn't want to talk about it, so I haven't been talking about it. That doesn't mean it's not happening."

"Oh. Okay. Well, I suppose it's fine by me if you want to see him again. You go ahead."

He's saying what I want to hear, but something isn't sitting right for me. It shouldn't be this easy, should it? "Is there anything we need to talk about first?"

"I said it's fine. You know the rules. As long as you stick to them, then there's no problem. I trust you. I just don't want to know about it beyond that."

The next few days I find myself questioning everything. Is he just saying yes because he feels like he has to? Surely he's a bit worried? Is he hiding it from me, or is he hiding it from himself and it'll all kick off when I'm on the date? Jonathan and I have been getting on so well lately. What am I doing? The easier it gets, the less I have to fight, the more my desire for this wanes. Do I just want what I can't have?

Jonathan seems more relaxed about all this than I am. I'm anxious about how the date will go, anxious about Jonathan's reaction when I get home, anxious that maybe I was just fighting to get my own way this whole time and maybe I don't really even want it.

Chapter 40

Lucy and I meet for a drink a few days before I'm due to meet Patrick. It's the first time I've seen her outside of her house without her wig on, or her signature red lipstick. She exudes less power than usual. But she looks more comfortable too. Stressed and tired, but like she's let down her safety net of smart clothes and makeup and is letting her true self shine through.

"Are you okay?" I ask.

She starts to answer, but the tears spill before the words get a chance.

I hug her and wait until she's ready to speak.

"After that night with you, I did a lot of thinking. I didn't want to tell Dave. I had fun with you, but I just wanted to pretend it hadn't happened and get back to my normal, simple life. But the harder I tried to ignore it, the worse it got."

I don't fully understand what she's saying. That she wishes we hadn't done it? Because she didn't want to, or because of what it's done to her and Dave, or because she misses my friendship? I understand it's caused her pain, but I hope she doesn't regret it. "I'm so sorry. We were drunk. We shouldn't have done it; it wasn't fair on you."

"No! I'm glad we did. It made me realise I'm gay. I haven't wanted sex with Dave for all this time because I'm gay, not because of him. I just don't want to be with a man at all. I'm not hiding who I am anymore, and that includes getting rid of my wig!"

All the soul searching I did after that night didn't really reach any conclusions for me. I still think of myself as straight—at least, mostly. But I can see the difference in Lucy, something deep inside her has changed. I am glad to have helped her discover this about herself.

"Wow! That's pretty huge news! You look awesome by the way, I like the new you."

She gives me a big smile and poses as if for a photo, her usual confidence shining through.

"Anyway, I realised I did need to tell Dave. It wasn't just about that night with us, it's bigger than that. There have been a few times in the past, before Dave too. I just thought it was youthful experimentation, but I was wrong. It's who I really am. Anyway, he didn't take it well. He's gone, moved out, and I don't know where. I haven't heard from him for three days now. He's made no attempt to contact the girls, either."

I reach out and squeeze her hand. "You've been so brave and honest with yourself and with him. Even if he doesn't like it, he should be there for you. I'm so sorry. I should've been there for you too. How can I help you now, with the girls or whatever you need?"

She gives me a big smile, and some of that strength and power I'm used to seeing in her shines through again. "It's okay. My sister is staying with us for a bit to help out. She's been great. I'm sure Dave will calm down soon enough and we'll work something out. It'll be okay."

She leaves to get back to her sister and the girls, my brain spinning in overdrive, thinking about that night, what it might mean for her marriage, and whether this means our friendship is back on track. Regardless of anything more than that between us.

Chapter 41

Finally, Patrick and I meet for our day date: a walk in the forest. It's only a second date but it feels like I've known him forever. Any doubts I had about whether I really want this disappear as soon as I see him and feel so at home with him, my heart singing in my chest. I want to touch him, and have him touch me. I want to listen to him talk and talk. I want to know everything there is to know about him.

Patrick really knows his stuff—which tree is which, which birds we can hear singing. He's telling me how the trees are all interconnected via their roots and fungi, how they work together to support each other, a real community. It adds even more of a dreamlike quality to the forest, thinking about all that going on that we can't see, and makes me want to pinch myself to remind myself I'm really here, on a date with this gorgeous and interesting man in this gorgeous and interesting place,

I'm wearing a dress I bought with Lucy, a little pink sundress with tiny white embroidered daisies. The sun is shining through the trees, but this dress is too cold in the shade of the forest. It's worth it, though. I know how pretty it looks, especially in the dappled green light.

After about half an hour of walking, with him teaching me all about the forest and me trying to pretend to be as at one with nature as he is, he stops.

"Follow me," he says with a sly smile, and we venture off the path and further into the trees. Climbing over and under branches, I do my best to keep up and wonder what I was thinking, wearing this silly dress for a walk, its thin straps digging into my shoulders and my skin exposed to brambles and cold. I walk a little too close to a bush, and my hair gets caught on a spiky branch, which Patrick has to rescue me from. Although I feel embarrassed, it's worth it for the sweet look on his face as he sets me free.

Eventually we arrive at a small clearing, which he seems to decide is the perfect place to stop.

And I can't argue. It's beautiful. We're surrounded by tall trees, moss and ivy climbing their gnarly trunks and carpeting the ground. Bright beams of sunlight flow down all around us between the trees. A single fallen tree, the one which must've created the clearing in the first place, lies across the middle, covered in ivy and fungi, home no doubt to millions of creatures. I lift a loose chunk of bark and watch as woodlice scatter in every direction.

Whilst I explore the clearing, Patrick takes off his bag, pulling out a blanket, a thermos of tea, sandwiches wrapped in tin foil. A real "dad" bag, but his practical preparedness is attractive. I feel looked after by him, and safe.

"I did a photoshoot here once. It's such a great spot, I've been meaning to come back here for ages."

He pushes my hair gently behind my ear and leans in to kiss me softly, behind my ear, then moves along my jawline toward my mouth, his breath hot on my cheek. He kisses my lips and then travels down my neck and chest, shivers of pleasure running through my spine. I've never felt so much like a fairy princess in my life. I felt light as air, as if I'd float away on the breeze if he didn't hold me down.

We sit on the blanket, which muffles the feel of the uneven ground below better than I expected it to, and start kissing again, his hand resting on my leg. My pussy is aching for him, and I quiver and bite my lip as he runs his hands up my thigh and under my dress. He uses both hands to pull my dress slowly up over my head. I kick off my pants and shoes.

I'm naked. Stark naked. Outdoors. In public. In the forest. This is new, and I think I like it. The cool air on my skin, the light from the sun shining through the leaves on the trees above, making patterns on my body like I'm in a swimming pool. I feel free in a way I don't think I ever have before. Patrick tilts his head to the side and lets out a sigh as he examines me in more detail than I think anyone has ever looked at me before.

"You're gorgeous like that. Can I take your picture?"

"Okay." I smile at him. "What do you need me to do?"

"Just stay where you are. And relax."

He pulls a camera out of his bag and takes a few pictures, climbing on the fallen tree to find the right angle. I feel self-conscious having his full attention on me, especially whilst I'm naked and he's dressed, but when he looks through the pictures and lets out a little groan of pleasure, I forget all about self-consciousness and feel like a sexy fairy princess again.

Once he's satisfied that he's got what he wants, he comes to join me. We lie there together for a moment, and I finally understand what people mean when they talk about mindfulness. I'm completely here, every one of my senses tuned in to my surroundings. My ears listening not for people who might spot us, but to the birds, the leaves rustling in the wind. I notice all the fresh, natural smells and the feel of the soft blanket, even with sticks poking up beneath it. It's so peaceful and beautiful. I could stay here like this forever with him.

Lost in the moment, I don't realise Patrick has moved until I feel his mouth on me. He covers me in a series of tiny, agonising bites, making my whole body come alive, before kneeling by my side and suddenly teasing his tongue across my clit. One flick of that tongue is all it takes for me to cry out in ecstasy, my hips flinging themselves toward him. He gives me an accomplished smile and raises an eyebrow before going back in for more. I lie back with a smile and I'm in heaven.

With his fingers deep inside me and his tongue moving fast, I come. I can feel it in every part of my body, from head to toe. I shake as he licks all over my body and then breathes warm air over me; it's pure bliss, the longest orgasm of my life.

But I'm still hungry for more. I reach out for his cock, still tucked away in his Levi's, but he shakes his head.

"Next time," he tells me, making me smile at the knowledge that there will be a next time. I store this memory for the quiet, lonely moments I feel sure will come when I start to doubt his interest. "You're cold," he says, rubbing the goosebumps on my arms, which are now almost purple under the greenish light, and hands me his soft bottle-green jumper as he reaches for the thermos and sandwiches. I pull it awkwardly over my head, emerging from its darkness like a dazed and confused turtle, my hair somehow all over my face and stuck in the collar. I reach up to sort my hair out, but Patrick gets there first. That sweet expression is on his face again as he pulls my hair out, off my face, and behind my ear, and then kisses me on the forehead and nose.

179

I lie back on the blanket and gaze up at the leaves silhouetted against the blue sky, listen to the breeze as it gently rustles the leaves together. It's so peaceful here.

I pull my phone out and make a video looking up at the sky and the leaves moving in the breeze, catching the sounds of the birds. "Ethel is going to love this!"

"Who's Ethel?"

"The lady I visit in a care home. She loves birds, but it's been a long time since she's been out in a forest. She just stares out at the same old view every single day now."

He looks at me now with such affection, his eyes almost sad. "You're so fucking lovely," he says with a smile, kissing me.

Chapter 42

I come home from the forest and head straight to the shower, as agreed. But this time Jonathan is waiting for me when I emerge. He grabs my still-wet body and pushes me playfully onto the bed and fucks me into oblivion, allowing me to let out the loud orgasm I kept quiet in the forest. I love feeling reclaimed like this, like he's marking his territory, reminding me how intimately he knows my body and what to do with it. Since Ben, it's like a tap has been loosened inside me and now Jonathan makes me squirt most times, leaving me breathless with pleasure. I often end up sleeping on a towel now.

As he slumps back onto the bed, I look at him properly for the first time since I got back. There's a quiet sadness to him that I haven't seen before.

"Are you okay?"

"Sarah has a new boyfriend. And he doesn't like her seeing me."

What? I can understand people finding the whole multiple-partners thing difficult, but Jonathan and Sarah are strictly platonic. They mean it when they say they're "just friends." This new boyfriend of hers sounds ridiculous and controlling;

surely she knows better than to accept something like this? "But that's crazy! There's nothing going on between you two! What's wrong with him?"

Jonathan cheers up a little at my reaction. "I know. He's got himself worked up over nothing. I just can't believe she'd stand for it."

"I'm so sorry. She's been so good for you. Are you worried about her? He sounds pretty controlling to me—I'm not sure that's good news."

"I hadn't thought of it like that. But no, she still seems like herself. I think she's happy, and she's got lots of friends around her to look after her. She's asked me not to contact her again so I need to respect that, not go on some crusade to try and split them up—I'd only be proving him right then, wouldn't I?"

"Okay, if you're sure. Well, how about you and I go cycling together at the weekend now that you've lost your biking buddy? It'll be fun!"

And we do. Not as far as he would go with Sarah, but we have a great day together just the same, cycling along the canal where it's nice and flat and I feel safely distant from cars. We haven't done anything like this in so long, I've forgotten how much fun we can have together when we're not doing DIY or talking about polyamory. I'm angry with Sarah for giving him up so easily, for not fighting harder. He loved spending time with her so much, and she's re-energised him in a way I don't think I ever could have. He's got into cycling because of her, been promoted at work because of her. And she enjoyed spending time with him too, as far as I could tell. This has got to be hurting her as much as him. I just hope her new boyfriend is worth it.

Sarah helped Jonathan to understand me; if it weren't for her, we would probably have split up, or be together but miserable. She saved us, and I'll always be grateful to her.

I don't want to lose her any more than Jonathan does.

Chapter 43

After I cancelled visiting Ethel with Frank so I could see Patrick, we realised it makes more sense for me to visit her alone once a week, to give Frank a bit of a break and Ethel some extra time with visitors. It's different visiting her on my own. I used to just sort of loiter in the background, but now I really need to engage with her; there's no one else to hide behind.

At first it feels quite awkward and difficult, but soon we find our way to each other through the birds. Frank and I often sit watching the birds from his house, so I ask the care staff to move a bird bath closer to Ethel's window so she can see them properly. She may have forgotten basic things like the way around her own home, but she knows her birds all right. She points out robins, blackbirds, goldfinches, sparrows, and blue tits, often spotting them far earlier than I do or hearing their song before she sees them.

Over time, she starts to open up to me more. Sometimes she knows where and when it is, and other times she's more confused, stuck in a memory. On the whole, these seem to be happy childhood memories and instead of feeling sad for her, I realise she's enjoying revisiting them, getting another chance

184

to feel like a child. Who wouldn't want that?

She whispers conspiratorially to me about staying up late last night, listening to the grownups talking and laughing in the next room, the smell of cigarette smoke coming under the door. It feels like a sign of how much she's come to trust me that she wants to share her secret with me. Those childhood secrets are so valuable. Another time, she's more agitated but it's still over a happy memory. A pilot has given her his jacket at the end of a dance, and she doesn't know how to reach him to return it.

Since the cooking course with Mum, I've really got into baking and often bring cakes with me to the care home, or to Frank. I've been doing more in the kitchen at the café too, giving Julie a break and a chance to chat more with the customers. She's been stuck back in the kitchen for so long, the regulars feel honoured to get her time and attention now, and she loves it too.

I invite Lucy to join me at the care home, and she even brings her girls along with her sometimes, much to everyone's delight. She's doing much better now; Dave has moved back in, and they seem determined to find their way to happily co-parenting, possibly even still living together whilst they work out what's next for them.

Everyone is particularly cheerful today because the hair-and-nails girls have been in to pamper all the residents. Ethel is sporting bright purple nails with glitter in them and has got the girls enthralled. The girls are sitting in the lounge showing their picture books to Ethel and a couple of other residents, giving Lucy and I a chance for a quick catch-up as we make cups of tea for everyone. As we busily pour the kettle and plate up the biscuits, our arms brush against each other and I feel a spark of electricity between us, a sudden desire to grab her and kiss her right there in the kitchen. I need to focus and remember where we are and what's going on.

"How are things with Dave?" I ask.

"Now that the expectation or hope of sex is gone, the pressure and frustration is gone too, and we're both much more relaxed with each other. He keeps talking about this promotion he's up for, though, possibly moving away to Dubai. I don't know what that would mean for the rest of us."

I squeeze the handle of the kettle more tightly. Dubai? She can't leave for Dubai! She can't let him go on his own, though, and leave the girls here. He's so close to them, but surely she doesn't really want to go? The realisation of how much I'd miss her hits me all at once and I know I really do want her to be more than a friend. Maybe it's time to start thinking of myself as bisexual, after all.

Lucy needs my friendship whilst she finds her way and finds the right path for her family, and I'm determined to keep good boundaries with her until she's worked that out. I don't want to make things even more difficult for her. I can't offer her a family life or monogamy, and that's what she really wants. If she's going to be in an imperfect relationship, it should be the one where her children get both their parents full-time, not some part-time thing with someone who's not even sure of their sexuality.

This thought leaves me feeling a little flat, but proud of myself too for doing the right thing and supporting her. If we're supposed to be together, it'll happen when the time is right. If I rush in too fast now, I could ruin everything, not just for myself but for Lucy and her family too.

Chapter 44

One Tuesday, Frank doesn't come into the café. He's become such a regular by now that the other customers notice his absence too. After the third person asks after him, I start to worry. Closing time can't come soon enough, and I rush through the jobs at the end of the day and leave in an equal hurry to walk to his house.

A cold feeling flows through my body and gives me a sense of dread as I walk toward that pretty door, which is confirmed to be correct as a tall man I recognise as his son opens it, his face ashen.

"Dad had a stroke in the night. He's dead."

I stop in my tracks. I want to ask a thousand questions, but I don't feel like I can speak properly.

"Would you like to come in?"

I follow him through the familiar honeysuckle-framed doorway and into the kitchen. It feels different already, the heart and soul of the house gone. "I'm Sophie, by the way. I work at the café round the corner. I come and visit Frank here sometimes, and your mum too. They're both so lovely."

He manages to dredge up a smile from behind the grief and shock which stains his face. "I'm Andy. And I thought it must be you. Dad has told me all about you. You've helped keep him busy since Mum went into that home. You've made his last months happier and easier on him. And on me and Mike too. We don't visit as much as we should, but it's helped take some of the pressure off knowing you were around. Thank you."

"It's a pleasure. We have a good time. At the moment, your mum is teaching me about all the garden birds she can see out of her window."

"Really?" He smiles. "She always used to try and teach us about the birds when we were younger, but I could only ever remember the sparrows and robins. I think she was a bit disappointed not to be able to pass on her love of nature to me."

I can't help but laugh at that. "She's definitely not disappointed in you. I've never heard parents talk so proudly about their children! If you want to know about disappointed parents, you should meet mine!"

"I'm sure they're proud of you too. Families are all complicated in their own ways, aren't they?" Andy looks down at the table and wipes a tear from his eye. "Dad made this table himself. He was always busy making something or other for the house. We used to put the sheets and blankets over it and make dens in here all the time, which used to drive Mum mad when she was trying to cook dinner!"

I stay for a little longer, having a cup of tea and chatting some more. But before long, I see the reality of what's happened hit Andy again, and he ushers me out so he can get on with funeral planning and all the other overwhelming things he's going to have to do now.

We close the café for the day of Frank's funeral a couple of weeks later. Julie, Amy, and I attend together, wearing bright colours as he requested. His sons have organised a beautiful service, sharing heroic tales of Frank's younger days that I would never have guessed at, but also confirming what a lovely, kind, and patient man he was. An involved dad, before it was expected of him, always ready to hear their stories even after a long day at work. Sadly, Ethel isn't well enough to be there for it, and probably wouldn't understand anyway. It is sad, but I'm also glad she's been spared of this experience.

Andy looks absolutely shattered, dark circles ringing his eyes, and confirms this to be the case as he tells me he hasn't been sleeping since his dad died. When he does sleep, he has dreams that Frank is still alive, trapped in the coffin and trying to get out. I don't know what to say. Frank had told me how claustrophobic he was, which Andy must know too, making those dreams all the more horrifying for him.

"He was so proud of you—they both were. He never stopped talking about you," I tell him, touching him gently on the forearm.

After the funeral, I call Jonathan and then my mum from the car, wanting to connect with my roots, to feel their stability, not staying on either call for long. It's too hot for a jumper, but Patrick's is there on the back seat, still not returned after our walk in the forest. I put it on and snuggle into it, inhaling the faint scent of Patrick, and feel safe. On the grass beside me a lone magpie is pecking at the ground, one for sorrow.

Despite only having known him for such a short time, Frank's death has had a real impact on me. It's like he and Ethel showed me what true love is, how it's supposed to go.

It makes me question, again, what I'm doing messing with Jonathan's heart, putting what we have at risk.

Chapter 45

I want to feel something other than sadness about Frank and Ethel. It's Jonathan's birthday tomorrow, so I decide it's about time I finally went through with the strip tease I planned for New Year's Eve. He's out for drinks with some of his friends from work, so I've got plenty of time to get myself ready to give him a surprise when he gets home later. I'm worried he'll think it's tacky and feel uncomfortable but I'm hoping that once we're both into it, he'll forget about that.

Whilst I'm in the hot bath, I get onto the internet, searching for videos that will give me stripping tips. I learn that his eyes will follow where I place my hands, so I need to make sure my hands are going to the places I want to show off. This tip is simple enough to give me the boost I need to believe I'll actually be able to do this.

I climb out of the bath, pour myself wine, and put on music as I get myself ready for what's to come. I plaster on far more makeup than I would normally find acceptable, foundation, red lipstick, eyeliner that grows thicker and thicker as I try to neaten it up, and three coats of mascara. I dance around the bedroom as I pull on a black velvet bodysuit with a slightly too small and over-padded bra to really push my boobs up and together. Fishnet stockings slip into ridiculously high heels. I check myself out in the mirror. I look really fucking hot!

I turn the music up a little and stay in front of the mirror, dancing. I want to see how I look, what works and what doesn't. I practice stroking my body, as per my online lesson, and it works; my eyes can't help but follow my hands. I practice sticking my ass out, putting my hands into my hair and swooshing it around. I feel sexy as fuck.

I can't wait for Jonathan to get home—I'm ready now. I video call Patrick, praying he'll be able to answer.

I sigh with relief when he answers and hold the phone away from myself so he can see me. I say nothing, and nor does he as he takes a moment to take in what he's seeing.

"Oh my god, you look incredible! What's the occasion?"

"It's Jonathan's birthday tomorrow. I'm going to dance for him."

"He's a lucky man. I wish I could be there."

"Maybe you'll get your turn one day," I tease, curling my hair around my fingers and biting my bottom lip.

After our call, I feel like a total seductress, powerful.

Jonathan arrives home, merry from his after-school drinks but not stupidly so, thank God. I shout hello and hear him making himself another drink and going into the lounge. When I think he's got himself settled, I follow him. He doesn't glance up from the TV until I turn it off and put on music. He's noticed now. His eyes are on stalks.

"Stay there," I instruct him. "No touching."

I start to sway to the music, running my hands up and down my body, through my hair. I keep my eyes on his, a suggestive smile on my lips at all times. He seems pleased and excited by what's happening, his eyes wide and a smile on his face, but I don't think he's entirely comfortable yet. I dance a little more extravagantly to try to make him laugh and relax a little. The dancing doesn't work, but me stumbling in my heels does the trick. We both have a little giggle at that, and I peel them off my feet as seductively as I can.

Both of us are more comfortable now. I come closer to him, leaning forward, my boobs in his face. This no-touching rule is hard but it's working, I'm desperate for him to touch me and can see how much he wants to. It feels amazing. Ben and Patrick have studied me like this, but I'm not used to feeling so desired by Jonathan.

His hand starts to go into his pants.

"You can't touch yourself, either. Not until I say so."

I turn around and, bending over, I slowly fold in half, sliding my hands down my legs so my ass is perfectly displayed for him in all its glory. My hands follow back up and around the soft velvet covering my ass as I turn back to face him and keep on dancing. I imagine Patrick is there watching me too and think about how turned on he's going to be when I tell him about this.

I go closer to Jonathan, kneel on the floor, and bring my face close to his lap, looking up into his eyes as I writhe around there, licking my lips. He's gazing back at me with a slightly dazed expression, like his brain has switched off and left his eyes and body in charge. This power is intoxicating! I feel like I could get him to do absolutely anything in this moment.

"You can touch me now," I whisper.

He pulls me in and kisses me hard, the smell of beer on his breath. His hands are all over me like he's never touched me before and might never get to touch me again. We hardly ever kiss in more than a polite way anymore; this is bliss.

He takes hold of me with a groan of pleasure and rolls me over to sit on the sofa whilst he kneels on the floor. The balance of power has shifted now, and he's going to have his way with me. I'm tingling with excitement as he undoes my bodysuit and peels off my fishnets before licking the tops of my thighs, tantalisingly close. His hands are still exploring my body, my ass, my tits, pulling me closer to him, his tongue moving to my clit at last, sending me wild.

"You taste so good," he mumbles into me, pausing to take a breath and starting to use his fingers too.

"Am I a naughty stripper? I'm not supposed to let you touch me. I'll be in trouble for this. Are you going to have to punish me?" Fuck! I don't know where that came from.

"You are a bad girl. Get on your hands and knees."

If I was shocked at myself just now, it doesn't come close to the shock I feel at hearing Jonathan like this, his sensible brain turned off and his body taking over at last. I do as I'm told.

He spanks me tentatively, but I want more.

"Harder!"

He obliges, and I cry out.

He starts to fuck me doggy style, bunching my hair up in his hand and pulling my head back. He's never fucked me this hard before; I didn't know he even wanted to do it like this. I'm not sure he knew, either. I'm pleased with myself for trying again anyway, not letting my fear of embarrassment get in the way. This has got to be the best sex we've ever had.

I'm really screaming out now as he comes with a deep shudder. I roll over onto my back and his hand goes to my pussy, rubbing hard until I squirt, liquid splashing up his arm and onto my belly.

He rolls to lie on the floor next to me, and I nestle in on top of him.

"Happy birthday," I whisper in his ear, kissing his neck softly.

Chapter 46

After feeding him chocolate cake for breakfast in bed the morning after my strip tease, Jonathan and I visit his parents for his birthday. They moved to the seaside when they retired a few years ago, so seeing them is always like a little holiday now. They're thrilled to hear about his promotion and what it means for him going into the new school year next month. Seeing them brings home to me what would be at stake if we were to split up, or if they found out what I've been doing. I know they wouldn't like the thought of their son's girlfriend sleeping with other men, or being (seemingly) unfaithful to their darling son.

The thought of being thrust out of their family is unbearable—they've been second parents to me since my awkward teenage days. I loved the normality of their family and home, with their Sunday roasts around the table. They didn't really understand my vegetarianism but his mum would always go to a great effort to make something special for me, so I could be part of their family meal. They ate around that table most nights, had real family conversations, played cards and board games—things we only did in my family on Christmas Day, usually ending in some kind of argument because one of my parents had got too drunk.

It felt like Jonathan had come along, my knight in shining armour, and introduced me to the normal life and family I craved. I just thought I'd end up like Mum, working too hard for too little, living on a council estate, probably a single mum, but Jonathan gave me my ticket to freedom. I'm grateful to him for our normal life that's so much better than the one I anticipated for myself, and once again I'm left feeling guilty that maybe that wasn't really what I wanted after all, that I tricked him into thinking I could give him that.

Jonathan's dad is fantastic, and I adore him. He looks just like Shakespeare, so much so that he's even done some modelling and impersonation work as Shakespeare over the years. He's just as great at storytelling too. Over dinner, he tells us about some of the people he's met recently since he's started volunteering to drive elderly people to their hospital appointments when they can't drive themselves. It makes me think of Frank and how much a service like this might have helped him.

"Lots of people, like us, retire and move here to be by the sea and they don't know anyone or have their families around. So, it's been a good way to meet people and to help people who I know really need it. Keeps me busy too!"

He's right. He was starting to lose himself since he retired and moved away, withering a little, his lovely spark dimming. Volunteering seems to have brought him back to life.

He tells us about the diabetic man who'd just found out he had to have his foot amputated, meaning his visions of playing football with his new grandson would never come true. He was distraught, and Jonathan's dad had been there for him, taking him home after the appointment and having a cup of tea with him before he left. I try to picture my own dad being so kind and thoughtful to someone he doesn't even know, but can't.

"Last week I met a lady who moved here to escape an abusive relationship. Two weeks after she moved here, she found a lump in her breast and found out she has cancer. She's got no-one; she can't even contact the people she knows at home because she's so scared of her husband. She's getting lots of help now from all sorts of agencies, but it's not the same as your friends and family, is it? And worst of all, because of her history, she's not even giving out her real name. It's like she's completely lost her identity. I'm just glad I've been able to do something to help her."

We're all quiet as we digest the sadness of this lady's situation.

Then Jonathan's dad goes on to tell another sad story about the two men in their eighties who have finally come out as a couple after decades of being in love. They'd both been married to women and had children and lived normal, respectable lives. They never lost contact with each other, apart from a brief period when they were so scared of HIV that they became more determined than ever to forget about their desire for each other. Both of their wives have died, and now they've moved in together and plan to marry each other in a small ceremony this Christmas.

It makes me realise how lucky I am, the privileges I have in being straight, never having had to deal with having to "come out" like Tom had to, or like Lucy will now. Because whatever this ends up being, I can always appear publicly to be in a "normal" heterosexual long-term relationship when I want and need to. And if rumours start, so what? Jonathan knows everything, so I'm not worried about that, and if people want to judge us, that's up to them. We know our real friends don't care; they've shown us that.

Whilst Jonathan and his parents are catching up, playing one of their games that I don't understand, I give Tom a call. To my great surprise, he answers.

"Hey," he says, and I can't help grinning at the sound of his voice with its New York twang. "How are you doing, sis? Are Mum and Dad okay?"

"We're all good. My friend has come out recently, and it just got me thinking about you and how shitty all that was."

"It all worked out okay. Being a gay teenager isn't meant to be easy. It's those things that make us stronger."

He's probably right. I certainly feel stronger in myself lately since I've stood up for what I want instead of just going along with what's expected of me, and it doesn't even come close to what he must've been through. "So how's life in the Big Apple? It looks amazing from your Instagram. I wish I could come and visit."

"Oh, Soph, it's amazing, but not like you think it is. My job sucks and I live in a fucking hovel. All those parties and things I go to are just work. I only go for the free food and beer."

"It still sounds glamorous to me," I say a bit pathetically.

"What's going on with you anyway?"

Now that's he's opened up to me about his situation, should I do the same? "Jonathan and I are good; we're doing up our house, trying to make it feel less like a new build. But it's not really working. And, also...we're trying out non-monogamy. I've got a sort-of boyfriend. And the girl who came out, I might have something with her too." I feel a burst of pride as I say this, and of hope that I'm right and not going to have to take it back next time I see him.

"Wow! You don't mess around, do you? Good for you, Soph. That's awesome. Have you told Mum?"

"Sort of. I tried, but she just shut me down, said she didn't want to hear about it."

"Ignorance is bliss, eh? She was the same with me—don't worry about it."

I go on to tell him more, even about what happened with Ben, which he reassures me is completely normal in the world of gay hook-ups and not something I should worry about.

Talking to Tom after so long is so comfortable. I'm determined to save up and go and visit him. No matter how much of a hovel he's living in, I want to see him.

Chapter 47

I'm glad to get away from home; Frank's death has hit me hard. I never had real relationships with my grandparents that I can remember properly. I've been sheltered, lucky not to have to deal with bereavement and grief before, and I feel like a fraud in my sadness now for stealing what belongs to his poor sons, who have lost one parent to death and the other to Dementia in such a short space of time.

We're always very well looked after by Jonathan's mum, and this trip is no exception. Stuffed full of his mum's cooking—many of the vegetables fresh from her own garden—we go out to try to walk it off. As we get closer to the beach, I spot the top of a Big Wheel. The fair is in town! My eyes are wide with excitement as I grab Jonathan's hand and start walking faster.

"Come on! Let's go on the fair!"

Reluctantly he follows, and soon we're sat high up at the top of the Big Wheel, enjoying the view of the town and the sea, glittering in the sunshine. It's higher than I thought it would be, and I find myself holding on to the cold metal of the safety bar tightly as I get a little rush of adrenaline.

"Do you remember when we all went camping for your

eighteenth birthday and we went on the Big Wheel together? It was just like this!" I said.

"I wanted to kiss you so bad. I had it all planned out, and it was going to be so romantic, having our first kiss up in the sky, but you wouldn't stop talking and it didn't happen!"

This revelation stops me in my tracks. My breathing slows as I look at him more closely and realise he means it. I never thought I was good enough for Jonathan, or anyone else, back then. I fancied him so much and we were friends, but he was older and much cooler and more popular than me, always strutting around school in a Nirvana T-shirt with a guitar on his back. I remember feeling bad for him that he'd ended up with me on the Big Wheel rather than one of his real friends, and talking incessantly out of nerves, but maybe he'd engineered it that way on purpose all along? "Really? I had no idea you were into me back then. I thought it was all the other way round. You should've done it!"

He smiles at me, a big, toothy grin and a glint in his eye, and then leans in to kiss me. A truly magical kiss up here so high, the noise of the fair distant below us. It makes up for that missed first kiss and I feel drunk with love.

Holding hands, we come off the Big Wheel, I'm feeling more in love with Jonathan than ever.

His hand reaches into his jeans pocket for his phone. There's a text from Sarah, which I spot as he opens it: *Happy Birthday. I miss you xx*

It's sweet that she's remembered it, but I'm still angry with her for abandoning him. He looks at the message and slips his phone back into his pocket without replying. Like with Ben, I tell myself I'm disappointed she's gone from Jonathan's life, but also grateful for what she's done for him and for our relationship. I'm not sure we'd have made it without her.

"Do you think you'll see Sarah again?" I ask.

"I'm not sure. I think she wanted more from me. Even though we didn't have any sexual chemistry, I think she still thought of me as a boyfriend. That's what she wanted, really, and now she's got it, hasn't she? It was confusing for us both and I think that's why he couldn't understand it, and it was easier to push me away rather than trying to."

This is the first time he's spoken about this with me, and I'm pleased he's opened up, but don't want it to ruin our fun. I pull him onto the Dodgems, where we seek each other out and smash our cars together as we laugh manically. I haven't had this much fun in ages! It's like I'm back on that trip again, drunk on cider, spinning on the Waltzers until I was sick. Jonathan was so sweet, rubbing my back and holding my hair, taking me back to the tent and nursing me through my first-ever hangover. It was the first time I felt truly cared for by him; I can still picture the sweet look of concern on his face.

That was the greatest summer. The summer Amy and I really got to know each other properly. No school, no homework, only a few hours of work each week, no stress, just spending all our time together before she and Jonathan went off to university, leaving me with another year to go at school.

As we make our way off the Dodgems, I grab his arm and squeeze myself tightly into him. "Do you remember that summer before you went to university? We had so much fun! God, and then I missed you so much when you went away. I was pining for you the whole time—it was awful!"

"I missed you too. It was strange being without you after we'd been together so much that summer."

I go a little quiet, wondering whether he cheated on me; he

must've been tempted to. There must've been opportunities. We even broke up for a few awful weeks at the start because he was worried he wasn't getting the "full experience." But I don't care; it doesn't matter. We love each other and we're happy, and that's all that matters.

I'm having a great time, but it makes me want to take the next step with Patrick, despite the thoughts I've been having about Frank and Ethel and what true love means. I'm at risk of breaking the spell of this weekend together, but I can't hold it in, and I want to take advantage of his good mood.

"Do you think I could spend a whole weekend with Patrick?"

Chapter 48

The four of us arrange to meet before Patrick and I go away together: Patrick and Kate, Jonathan and me. We figured that this way, we'll all feel a bit awkward and uncomfortable, so it's fair. No one has the upper hand. After some discussion, we've decided to go to their house for dinner—as with meeting Ben, it removes any risk of us being spotted and having to come up with an explanation for how we all know each other. And it saves them from having to organise a babysitter too.

Jonathan and I have a conversation about boundaries and expectations before we go. I want to make sure he's considered all the possible outcomes and is prepared for them. I want to know what he's open to and what he isn't—if he fancies Kate, would he want to do a swap? He looks shocked at the mere suggestion of this and clarifies that he just wants this meal to be a normal meal, two couples having dinner. I'm not surprised, but I'm a little disappointed. It would be so perfect if Jonathan and Kate did fancy each other—it would all be so much easier if it were even and he had someone else too—but if he's already decided he's not even open to the idea of being attracted to her, then there's no chance of that, and certainly no chance of us all playing together, although I'm not sure how I'd feel about that anyway.

Walking up to their front door, I've got butterflies in my stomach, far worse than when I've met Patrick before. I'm worried Jonathan won't like Patrick and won't want me to see him again, or that Kate won't like me and won't want me to keep seeing Patrick. I'm worried I'll be different with Patrick in front of Jonathan, that he'll see me in a new light and not want me anymore. Jonathan seems completely relaxed though. I'm glad he's okay, but it's a little unnerving too.

Kate answers the door looking effortlessly dishevelled, brown hair bouncing and tumbling from her head and wearing a loose-fitting black dress and big silver jewellery, a stack of bracelets jangling on her wrist. "Come on in," she says with a huge smile.

We walk into the house and follow Kate through to the large, immaculate kitchen. It's all shiny white cupboard doors, shiny black worktop, an island as big as our entire kitchen. It's not to my taste at all, but I know Jonathan will be in complete awe at the size and cleanliness of it.

"What a beautiful home," I say to Kate as I hand her the £7 bottle of wine I felt fancy buying on the way over here, but which seems woefully inadequate now I've seen their home.

"Thank you. I find it a bit ridiculous, having all this space. It's a bitch to clean."

"I bet! Not my favourite hobby!"

"Me neither. We have a cleaner, but I still feel like I'm cleaning constantly. I hate it. I wish we could be in an older, shabbier house, really, one where dirt and mess adds character rather than making everything look awful."

A cleaner? That's been a lifelong dream of mine, one I always thought was completely unrealistic. I feel a little out of my depth here in this perfect, shiny house.

Patrick has taken a couple of beers out of the fridge and he and Jonathan have gone into the lounge, where I can hear them getting stuck into the safe topic of football immediately—with plenty of World Cup stories and opinions to share, they'll be fine. That leaves me and Kate to get to know each other. She's just as lovely in real life as I hoped.

Eventually I feel brave enough to ask what I really want to know. "So how did you guys end up opening up?"

"Pat was working away a lot, and often with beautiful models. I'd been cheated on before and I couldn't handle it. I was getting really jealous and paranoid it was going to happen again. In the end I realised it was just easier to open up, to trust him to make sensible decisions that wouldn't hurt me or the kids and to be honest about them, rather than to try to trust him never to be interested in anyone else."

Kate tells me how hard it is to get a babysitter, how hard it is for her and Patrick to have a full night away together, to just be a couple and not have to be responsible parents for a bit. How it's got even harder now her mum is too sick to help out and she's having to give more of her time to care for her too, and her dad is finding it hard and needs a lot of support. Plus, she still has the kids, and work...

But then she starts to tell me about some of her dates, and it's like a light has been lit inside her. She comes alive, suddenly more animated and smiling, her eyes shining bright. "Dates are an escape where I get to just be myself, to feel sexy and wanted, rather than needed. I love pampering myself before a date. Even that nervousness is so exciting."

"Me too. Getting ready is almost as fun as the date!"

We're both smiling widely as we talk more about dates.

She continues, "The pleasure I get on the date is more than enough to offset any feelings of guilt I have about not being with Mum or the kids in that time. I'm sure it makes me a better mum, wife, and daughter in the end."

I'm nodding away at her. It's so good to hear this, that she can see that the benefits are so much more than sex too. "I definitely feel like a better person since we've opened up. I'm much more motivated to exercise and eat healthily, and I think Jonathan and I are getting on better now than we used to. And I've been getting on better with my mum than ever before too." I just hope Jonathan can see all this too.

"Pat and I are happier now I'm not being paranoid and jealous. I think a little bit of healthy competition helps keeps things interesting between us, so we don't take each other for granted."

"Definitely! I don't think Jonathan ever considered that anyone else might be interested in me, so he never worried about me leaving him for someone else before. He's realised he has to up his game now though! So how much do you actually do it? Sorry, I feel like I'm interviewing you here! It's just so interesting to meet other people who do this."

She laughs at this. "It's okay! We don't do it much, really, once every few months. Pat went a bit crazy at first, testing the boundaries a bit, I guess. For me, just knowing I could do something, that my options are open, is enough most of the time."

I can see that. I think that's how Jonathan feels too, but I still hope he'll act on it again someday.

Next, I ask the big question. "Do you get jealous?"

"Not really. I don't generally want to know what he's been

up to beyond that something has happened, and it was safe. Ignorance is bliss as far as I'm concerned. Pat likes to hear all the gory details about me with other guys, though. It really turns him on."

I catch myself just in time before agreeing with this statement. She's just told me she doesn't want to hear what he's doing with other people, and that includes me.

Kate takes a pause, and a more serious expression comes over her face. Her eyes flicker and her fingers play with the stem of her wine glass. Her voice is quieter and more monotone as she tells me, "This is new, though. It's always just been sex before. We've never really told each other much about other people we've met, and we've certainly not even considered introducing them to each other. I was really nervous about tonight."

Wow! I was under the impression they were always out on dates with other people, all playing together and having a great time. I wonder if Patrick has introduced me to Kate because he feels something more for me than the others, or if it's because I pushed it, or maybe just that I'm the first local person he's met and the rest were when he was working away. Either way, he didn't have to, and I'm glad he did. If I was after some reassurance that he really likes me, then I just got it!

Kate goes on to explain how she loves both her children equally, knowing she has plenty of capacity for love within her, so if more children or partners come along, she knows she has room to love them too, each in their own way. I've spent so long thinking about and trying to explain to Jonathan how me having feelings for someone else doesn't mean I love him any less, but I've never thought of it in this parental way before. Over the last few months, I've felt so much closer to my parents, and I finally feel like they love me and are proud of me, and it's in a different way to how they love Tom. We don't need to compete for their love; they have enough for both of us, even if it doesn't always feel like it.

The doorbell rings, and Kate goes dashing off, so I join in the boys in the lounge. I don't know how to be with either of them in front of the other. I want to touch them both, but I'm worried how that might make the other feel. I'm second-guessing everything I say, trying to make sure I give them equal attention, don't laugh more at one's jokes. It's ridiculous.

Kate returns, armed with three large takeaway pizzas. My mouth is watering at the delicious smell alone.

"Sorry, it's been manic today. I had all these plans for dinner, but everything kept going wrong. So much for the vegan thing—these are all veggie, though. I hope that's okay?"

"Course it is. Who doesn't love pizza?"

After being so blown away with the perfection of their home, it's reassuring to see how normal and human Kate is. I really like her.

We stay in the lounge, pizza boxes strewn across the floor, munching away happily. Kate starts asking Jonathan questions, and soon I'm deep in conversation with Patrick, barely aware the other two are with us.

Dinner passes without a hiccup, everyone chatting away like we've known each other forever and have years of happy memories behind us. It feels like all my dreams are coming true.

As we come to the end of the night, my attention is drawn back to Kate and Jonathan, and I wonder if I can see the hint of a spark there. A spark that, despite how happy he was in her company, I didn't see between him and Sarah. I haven't dared even hope for this, for fear of disappointment. He's told me he's monogamous, he only wants me, and I respect that. But maybe, just maybe, he's tempted. God, I hope so. I just wish it felt more equal, that he could feel some of what I feel and better understand how exciting it is, but also how much it makes me love him.

It's really attractive, seeing Jonathan like this, flirty and relaxed. Kate is completely engaged in the conversation, laughing at his jokes, and it makes me realise just how much I love him, what a great catch he is. He seems hotter, funnier and more interesting from this slight distance.

As we leave, I watch Patrick and Kate holding each other as they wave us off, backlit in the doorway. They look so comfortable and in love, and it makes my heart feel warm and fuzzy. It's good seeing them so happy together and reassures me I'm not about to cause a divorce or be branded a home-wrecker.

Tucked up in bed with the lights off when we get home, Jonathan and I discuss the evening.

"Did you like them?" I ask.

"Yes, they're both lovely, aren't they? It feels better now I know he's a good guy, and that he and Kate are happy together. It puts my mind at ease."

"So can we do the weekend away?"

He closes his eyes and takes a breath. I feel like I can see the cogs turning in his brain as he tries to picture me going away and how he'll react. "Yes. That actually sounds less daunting than what we've done tonight. I still don't like it or want it, and I don't want to hear anything about it, but you can go. I just want you to be happy."

Although I was confident that he'd say yes after going to all the trouble of meeting Patrick, it still feels such a relief to hear him say it so clearly at last. "I can't be happy if I'm making you miserable, though. Ask me questions, give me rules, whatever you need to do to make it easier."

"You need to accept that I'm never going to be completely happy with this. But I am going to do my best."

"Okay. Thank you. I love you."

I kiss him and snuggle into his warm, familiar body, wishing he could get more on board with this, actually welcoming it because he can see that it's good for us both, instead of just accepting it and going along with it.

Chapter 49

"Everything okay?" I ask hesitantly. Jonathan has been on the phone with his mum for ages. They're close, but they don't usually chat away on the phone like that. He is a little pale, clearly shellshocked.

"Everything's fine. Dad had a bit of a funny turn in the garden centre this afternoon. He's in hospital, and they're doing some tests and keeping him in overnight just to be on the safe side. It's made them both face up to their mortality, so Mum wanted to talk through their Wills and stuff with me while they could."

"Wow! Must've been a difficult conversation. Is he okay now?"

"He's fine. Anyway, I don't really know how it started. I guess it was just an emotional call all round, but I told her about us opening up and meeting Patrick and Kate last week."

I'm speechless; I didn't see that coming. I can feel myself gently sweating, nervous about how the conversation went, what his mum thinks of me. "What did she say?"

"She let out a great hoot of laughter when I told her, said that from my tone, she was expecting it to be something awful. She's all for it—she started telling me some stories of her own from the seventies, but thankfully I was able to put a stop to that quickly."

Well, this is unexpected!

Although I knew she was older than my parents (Jonathan was a surprise arrival when she was forty-two and had given up hope of ever having a child) and just about old enough to be my parents' parents at a push, I didn't realise before Jonathan tells me now that she'd been married twice before she met Jonathan's dad. She claims that making monogamy a deal-breaker is what ended her first two marriages, and keeping the door open to it the third time round was their secret to success. (I can literally see Jonathan with his fingers in his ears and eyes closed, wanting the floor to swallow him up when she told him this!)

One of my main concerns about all of this was how his parents might react and turn against me, but now that they're on my side, I feel better about everything. I can't quite gauge if the conversation has changed Jonathan's views; I think he's still taking it all in.

I continue visiting the care home every Monday and start getting to know some of the other residents too, staying for slightly longer each time I go. Usually, I come armed with some of my baking experiments for the staff and residents, who are always appreciative. It's a pleasure spending time with them, hearing their stories and wisdom, the dreams they realised and didn't, the regrets they have, their love stories.

With some, I play card games or complete wordsearches and crosswords. I help others read letters from their grandchildren and help them compose replies. A sweet lady called Margaret tries and fails to teach me to knit, her lavender talcum powder smell transporting me back in time to when I was little and visiting my own grandparents, whom I barely remember. But mainly I sit with them and listen for as long as they want me to, often just sitting in comfortable silence. I learned from Frank how much that helps.

As I'm leaving one week, Wendy, the manager, pulls me to one side. I really like Wendy—she is so dedicated to her residents, does everything she can to make it feel like a real home. She has a friendly but always harried-looking face, the responsibility of so many people's lives weighing heavily on her shoulders.

"Sophie, we're going to be recruiting a new Activity Co-ordinator to work here. I'm putting the advert out today. You should apply; you'd be great at it."

I take an application form and tell her I'll think about it. But it doesn't take much thinking about—I love coming here. By the end of my walk home, I'm brimming with ideas for activities already. As much as I love working with Julie at the café, it feels like a temporary job, the kind of thing you do as a teenager on a Saturday. But I could actually turn this into a real career, bring my own ideas to life and genuinely make the end of those residents' lives happier.

I bump into Andy at the end of his visit with Ethel. He's looking much better now than at the funeral. Ethel is having a snooze, so we get chatting.

"How are you doing?" I ask him.

"Getting there."

"Have those dreams stopped?"

"They've changed. I had one last night actually. Dad was there, alive and well and in my house. It was nice, comforting, to feel like he was there and that everything was normal. But even in the dream, I knew we'd done the funeral already, so I was trying to work out how we were going to tell people he was back or whether I should just keep it secret and have him all to myself. It was so vivid."

I can't work out if that's terrifying or reassuring. "That sounds confusing, but maybe it means your brain is processing it all, so hopefully it's good news. You've been through so much over the last few months."

Suddenly, breaking news is announced on the TV, drawing us both in immediately. A plane has disappeared, all 298 people on board presumed dead, just four months after the same thing happened back in March, with 239 lives lost. Once again, the news is filled with distraught families wanting answers that no one seems able to give.

We both watch, mouths agape.

"How can this be possible? I've never heard of this happening before, and now twice in just a few months?"

"Those poor families. Dad was old and we know exactly what happened to him, and it's still screwed me up so much. Imagine not knowing what happened, or not being able to say goodbye. It's awful."

No goodbyes, no explanations, no closure. All those lives lost; the lives of their families destroyed too.

Chapter 50

L ying on my back, feet up against the wall and chatting away on the phone with Amy, I feel like Clarissa, my favourite nineties American teenager. All that's missing is the twirly phone cord wrapped around my fingers. I've not seen Amy since Frank's funeral, so I tell her about visiting the home and the job I'm applying for there. I tell her about meeting Kate, and how I think I saw a spark between her and Jonathan. And I tell her my plans for going away with Patrick, our first full night together, this weekend.

"Oh! And we went home for Jonathan's birthday and went on the fair! It was so much fun! Do you remember that camping trip the summer before you and Jonathan went off to uni?"

And before I know it, she's casually telling me how the two of them were a "sort-of" couple, "friends with benefits, really" at uni when we'd split up for those few awful weeks. She's telling me it in such a chilled-out, relaxed manner that I can hardly comprehend what she's saying. When Jonathan said he wanted to split up to have the full experience, I assumed he meant having sex with new people, not our existing friends. They've always been close, really close, but I thought it was in a brotherly-sisterly kind of way.

"It's such a relief to finally tell you, now I know you'll be okay with it," she's saying, breezy as anything. So breezy, I can't bring myself to contradict her.

I bring the call to a close and sit in a stunned silence. I don't know how I feel about this. I think back to that time when we'd split, driving around aimlessly in my first car, a beat-up Fiat Uno, crying, with no-one to talk to, my boyfriend and my best friend both gone, and Tom not far behind them, leaving me abandoned and alone.

She's right, I should be okay with it. I'd already assumed he'd been sleeping with other people when we broke up, and it should be better that it's someone I know and love, rather than some mysterious person I'll never know about.

So why am I so pissed off?

I know I can't stew on this forever; it'll eat me from the inside out. So, after a few deep breaths, I go straight to Jonathan. "Amy just told me about the two of you at university."

He goes pale. "I'm so sorry. I'm so sorry. It was only a friends-with-benefits thing, never anything more. I always knew you were the one. Amy and I are mates. We were lonely and lost there, and people seemed to think we were a couple because we spent so much time together and it just sort of happened." His eyes are wide with a mixture of hope and fear. He looks so sweet. I don't want to be angry with him; I've put him through enough. I need to forgive him for this.

I take a deep breath and imagine breathing out whatever hurt or anger I took in when I heard this news. "I get it. I was lonely too when you both left me. I had my friends and family around, but I was still lost without you both. It was awful. I do understand how it happened."

His shoulders fall in relief at this.

"But that doesn't make it okay that you've lied to me for so long about it. How could you? I feel so stupid! I wish she'd never told me."

"I just, I've felt so guilty about it for all these years, and I didn't tell you right away, and then it got harder and harder to do it. It's why I went along with this whole open-relationship thing at first, even though I wasn't really sure."

I can feel an explosion of anger rising inside me at this. How dare he turn this back on me when he's the one in the wrong? "That's not fair! Don't pretend you only did this out of guilt! You wanted to do it too at first—you still want the freedom now. If some hot girl came on to you tomorrow, you'd want to know you could go with it and enjoy it."

He gives a big, angry huff, which I think is entirely unreasonable, given how this conversation started. "Sometimes I wish you could've just cheated, and I didn't have to know anything about it."

What? I shake my head, unable to believe he's said that. "What the fuck? How could that possibly be better? You'd have found out in the end, just like I've found this out. I would hate hiding something from you that made me happy. I couldn't do it."

He nods at this and looks calmer, his normal self again. "I know. And I know that's a good thing. And I'm glad you can be honest with me; you're brave and I admire it. But it's so hard."

We both take a breath to calm down a bit.

"I really am sorry about Amy, and for not telling you sooner."

"I know. And I'm sorry too for all this. I know you don't want any of it, really."

He smiles at me, his eyes slightly damp. "You're right. I don't want it. I don't like it and I don't want to hear about it.

But I do accept it. I can see that you're happier now, and it does sort of take a pressure off me to be your everything. And I really like Patrick, and Kate, and Lucy too. But I wish I could make you that happy all by myself."

That hits me right in my heart and almost takes my breath away. I hold his hand and look right into his eyes. "You do make me happy—you make me really happy! You love me just the way I am, and I love you for it, but it doesn't make me stretch myself to be better and I want to be better, for myself and for you. And I know I can be a pain sometimes, and I want sex more than you do, so this can take some of that pressure away. It's better for you too."

"I know. I'm going to learn to be okay with this. Please be patient with me."

I look at him and know that we're okay, that we'll be okay. But I still feel angry at Amy, unfairly angry, given my forgiveness toward Jonathan.

I realise this is another turning point, a fork in the road where we can choose to forgive and forget or choose not to. It feels like a choice to be together, a choice we've made over and over, not taking the easy option or keeping the status quo. Knowing we could be with other people, people who might be hotter or younger or richer or smarter or funnier, forces us to keep working on our relationship and ourselves, and we're both better off for it. Jonathan has had to forgive me for a lot of difficult things over the last year or so; I can let this old fling go. And I'm away for the weekend with Patrick, so he's going to have plenty of time to stew on it, which is probably punishment enough.

"So, we're okay?" he asks.

"We're okay. I love you," I confirm.

"Love you too. Always," he says with a cheeky grin, knowing he can't fail to win me over with a Harry Potter reference.

Chapter 51

Legs aching, I lag behind Patrick up the hill on the coast path. We've been walking for about four hours under the blazing sunshine with only occasional shade. It's beautiful—blue sea to my left, green fields to my right. But the hills! They're relentless and unforgiving. Mum does a lot of walking these days and would be proud to know I was doing this, so it's a little disappointing that I won't be able to tell her about it—she made it clear enough that she doesn't want to know anything about this, and I don't think I could tell her about it without mentioning that I was here with another man.

I keep going, one foot in front of the other, blisters forming in my brand-new never-been-worn-before walking boots. We're almost at the top when I realise the top is not the top after all. There are a few hedges and trees hiding the true summit of this hill, which continues farther up. I think I'm going to have to give in and let him know how tired I am.

"Can we have a break?" I pant.

"Not yet. We're nearly there, I promise."

We keep walking; he's telling me about the geology of the cliffs here and how we'll soon see it change from sandstone to limestone. I'm not entirely sure how interested I am in rocks, but I could listen to him talk forever, no matter what the subject. I just love that voice and the knowledge and passion that shines through. Aside from anything else, I'm glad not to have to waste my valuable breath responding to him.

As we come to the top of the hill, we're greeted with the most beautiful view down onto a little cove. Big blue sky over big blue ocean. I take off my sunglasses and use my T-shirt to wipe my face, a mess of suncream and sweat. We walk down the hill, closer to the beach until we reach a treacherous-looking narrow, steep, rocky path down the cliff. Before I have time to think about whether it's safe or sensible, Patrick is confidently making his way down, and I have no choice but to follow.

I'm glad I'm behind him so he can't see my half-sitting scramble or my awkward facial expressions as I wince and hold on to tufts of grass and not-entirely stable rocks. The small trickle of water that must've initially created this pathway appears about halfway down, and I do my best to navigate around it and stay dry.

The path widens as I get closer to the beach, and I can walk normally. Looking up, I see Patrick taking his shoes off, sighing in relief as he stretches his toes out in the sand. I'm excited to follow suit; I can almost feel the pleasure of it already as I join him and sit down. As I start to undo the laces of my walking boots, he starts taking off his clothes.

"What are you doing?" I ask.

"Going for a swim. Coming?"

I stare at him in disbelief, knowing already that there's no point fighting this. I'm going in whether I like it or not.

I shake my head, laughing, as I start taking off my clothes. It's become a race, who can get naked and into the water first. Even with his head start, I'm determined to win this one.

Racing down the beach, I can feel him hot on my heels, but I know he won't catch me, and I like the thought of him watching my bare bum bouncing up and down, my hair flowing behind me. I use the run on the sand to try to mentally prepare for the next step. I don't swim unless I'm abroad, and even then, I'm happier at the side of the pool. But I'm going to do it. I'm going to dive in, embrace the cold, and not worry what the salt water will do to my carefully blow-dried hair.

My toes hit the water first and it's not so bad, it's going to be fine.

It is not fine. Any illusions I had of looking like I'm on *Baywatch* quickly disperse as I wince and wade in further, to my knees, my waist. Desperate to stop here, I fight my instincts and throw myself forward into the sea. It's icy cold and takes my breath away, but actually feels really good, liberating, after being in tight, sweaty clothes and boots in the sun all day.

There's a splash next to me as Patrick arrives and dives in himself. It only takes four or five strokes for me to swim to him and kiss him. He takes me in his arms, and the cold disappears. All that matters is this moment. I've never been with someone before who can draw in my entire energy like this, the rest of the world and its problems gone.

We swim a little, float on our backs, splash each other. I swim further out into the open sea than I ever have before, and I feel so free, completely naked, held by the water, no one else in sight but Patrick.

Soon the cold has seeped deep into my bones, and I need to get out. I race up the beach, suddenly aware of my nakedness. There's no one around on the beach, but it's impossible to tell if people are up on the coast path or not.

I pull two microfibre towels from Patrick's bag and wrap one around me, passing him the other as he returns. I twist my hair and wring out as much water from it as I can. The sun is warm, and I feel blissfully happy standing there naked but for the towel over my shoulders.

Patrick lays his towel out on the sand and lies down, beckoning for me to join him. I snuggle in next to him, pulling my own towel over me for a little privacy. I'm not as body confident as him. Turning onto our sides, we lie there quietly, just gazing at each other, enjoying the peace as we listen to the sounds of waves lapping at the shore and seagulls squawking above us.

"Aren't you worried someone will see us?" I ask.

"Doesn't it make it more exciting?"

No! It scares the hell out of me. I try to convey my feelings with a look but think it ends up being more of a confused sneer.

"I know about this place because I worked on an article for a magazine all about the decline of the British seaside and how no-one comes here anymore, so I think we'll be okay."

He kisses me gently, tasting vaguely salty from the sea, the power of his kiss an electric shock setting my body ablaze. I roll on top of him, my wet pussy resting on his stomach. His hands come to my waist, my tits, and up to my chin and face. The adoring way he looks at me! Like he can't get enough; he can't believe he's allowed to see me naked and touch my body. I feel like a princess, a mermaid.

I pull him up to sitting, me in his lap, and wrap the towel around us. I feel so warm and safe with him, the sun on my back. I kiss him and feel his cock, so close to me, hardening. I lift up and onto him, sliding my warm, wet pussy over him, and grind up and down. My face stays close to his, our breathing slow and deep, as though we are one. His hands are warm on my back, holding me close.

He buries his face into my chest, my nipple in his mouth as he sucks hard. I take a sharp breath at the pleasure of this. Throwing my head back, the towel falls from my shoulders, but I don't care. It's invigorating to be naked in such a beautiful place. His finger moves to my clit and he strokes it, in rhythm with his tongue flicking across my nipple.

He pushes me onto my back and lies on top of me, thrusting his cock in and out, in and out. My breathing becomes even deeper as he comes with a shudder, still inside me as we lie back onto the towel, pulling the other over us too.

We lie there in silence, looking at each other waiting for our breathing to return to normal. I'm utterly captivated by him. I don't want to leave this moment ever.

We doze off blissfully on the beach for a while longer, listening to the waves and the seagulls, his body warming mine after the cold of the sea. Then we put back on our sweaty clothes and boots and continue with our walk—another hour, and we should be back at the B&B.

On my way back to the path (which impossibly seems even more precarious from the bottom) I pick up a pretty shell. My thumb fits inside its smooth centre perfectly, a memento of this day.

Chapter 52

Finally in the B&B room after demolishing a big bag of salty chips on the seafront, we chill out on the big bed—its floral linen and carpet clashing perfectly with the curtains—offering each other sleepy smiles. I snuggle into Patrick, inhaling the salty smell of the beach and sweat from the day. This contented feeling is addictive, and it's tempting to fantasise about what it would be like to be with him full-time.

I have to remind myself it wouldn't always (or even often) be like this. There's his kids, his work and mine. I remind myself that if we were together all the time, it couldn't be special things like this all the time. We'd argue about the washing up just like any other couple. He hasn't seen me hung over, sick, without makeup, with PMS and all the other things Jonathan sees and supports me through all the time; Patrick only knows me at my best, and I like it that way. It's only so good with Patrick because it's an occasional treat. I can't—I mustn't—compare this to the unconditional love I've shared with Jonathan for so long.

I jump in the shower to wash away the sea, sex, and sweat of the day, the cold water a shock on my slightly sunburnt skin.

I'm daydreaming, remembering the rush of getting naked and running into the sea.

Lathering shower gel up my thigh, it hits me: we didn't use a condom. Fuck! I stay in that position, leaning forward, hand on my thigh, jaw clenched tight, water rushing over me as I go over every moment to confirm what I already know.

I turn off the shower, wrap a towel around myself, and walk dripping into the bedroom. "We didn't use a condom there on the beach."

"No." He seems unconcerned.

"It's one of our rules. We have to use a condom."

"I know, but we can't change it now. Don't get upset. I've had a vasectomy; you won't get pregnant."

"It's not just that, though."

"You got tested before we met, right? And you've been using protection the rest of the time? Me too. You don't need to worry about this."

But worry I do. I've betrayed Jonathan's trust. And Kate's. And whilst I did use condoms with Ben, Lucy and I didn't use anything. I think that's okay, and she's obviously not been sleeping with anyone else except Dave, but I'm not really sure if it's as safe as I think it is. No one taught us about that at school.

I feel angry with Patrick for not taking charge and doing the right thing, although it is of course just as much my fault as his. I know he's right, but I still have to decide whether or not to tell Jonathan, and I want Patrick to understand that and take it more seriously. This is our first night together, and I'm at risk of ruining it. Am I just making a mountain out of a molehill? I decide to let it go for now. I can't change anything anyway.

Chapter 53

Despite our tiredness from a full day's walking in the sun, we stay up late into the night talking. I want to get right into his head, to know *every single thing* about him, want to tell him *every single thing* about me. I never had this discovery time with Jonathan; we grew up together, and there wasn't much left to tell that we didn't already know. That was beautiful too, to feel so completely safe with someone, but it feels incredible to have this time now, to feel Patrick hanging on my every word.

The same goes for our bodies. It's the first time we've been together like this, alone in a private room. However secluded our exciting outdoor adventures have been, there's always been an element of rush to get some clothes back on, to not push our luck and risk getting caught.

Tongues and fingers take their time to explore every nook and cranny now, though, kissing behind ears, along collar-bones, the backs of knees. He slowly moves all the way from my bum to my head, kissing every notch of my spine as he goes. Every inch new and exciting, every inch alive with pleasure and the anticipation of more to come.

He flips me onto my back and grabs and kisses me hungrily,

licking all the way up my legs. "You're delicious!"

I'm panting with desire, desperate to feel him inside me.

He pushes my legs up, and I hold my knees up to my shoulders. He leaves me waiting in that position as he makes a big show of putting a condom on (which I try not to roll my eyes at) before fucking me deep and hard. I cry out in pleasure.

He flips me over, pulls my hips up into the air to fuck me hard and fast, my face squashed into the pillow and his hands big and warm on my ass. I can feel him losing control and I love feeling so powerful, like he can't help but fuck me harder and harder.

Not wanting to finish yet, he slows down, pulls out, and rolls me onto my back. His face has a sheen of sweat over it, which makes me smile, but my smile drops instantly when a horrifying squelch emerges from my vagina as a rush of air escapes.

My whole body tenses up, eyes wide with shock and panic. "Fuck, oh my god, sorry, that's so embarrassing," I start burbling away, but Patrick just laughs and snuggles into me.

"You're so cute," he says, giving me a little squeeze and a kiss before rolling on top of me again.

He fucks me more slowly now, his face close to mine, his breath on my neck. I wrap my legs around him, pull him closer and deeper into me. It feels more intimate and private like this, more real. Finally, he allows himself to come, with an intense shudder that seems to go on and on.

We disentangle from each other and lie there, just gazing at each other as we drift off to sleep. I want to push up into his body, squeeze him tight, but I'm uncertain how he'll react. I don't want to scare him off. But then an arm is lazily thrown across my body, pulling me into his warmth, and I glow with how easy and comfortable it feels.

Suddenly we're not falling asleep anymore, and his breath is warm on my face as he looms over me. Moving slowly, feeling every part of our newly discovered bodies moving together, we fuck ourselves into a long, deep, satisfying sleep, a sweaty tangle of arms and legs.

I wake up in the morning and make my way to the bathroom, where I get a bit of a shock when I look in the mirror. My hair was obviously still wet from the shower when I fell asleep and is now an enormous curly straw bird's nest. Craning my neck down, I run water over my hair and attempt to tame it a little before pulling it into a plait. That'll have to do for now.

"You are adorable in the morning," Patrick says when I return, holding the covers up to make room for me to climb back into his warm, waiting arms. "Shall we get room service for breakfast?"

He reaches for the phone and places our order—two vegetarian full English breakfasts with no eggs, and then snuggles back into me and we doze off again.

When the knock on the door comes, he wraps a dressing gown around himself and collects our food, taking it out to the little balcony overlooking the sea. I climb out of bed and reach for my dressing gown, but he shakes his head at me and takes his own back off. "Let's eat naked!"

Sitting out there with him, both of us naked, eating our breakfast, just about able to hear the sea, I feel so content. After breakfast, we return to bed and stay there, kissing, cuddling, and having slow morning sex, until the very last moment possible before we have to get dressed and check out. This is bliss; everything I've been hoping for. A lazy, unrushed morning together. It sounds so simple, but it feels so impossible to achieve. I've given up on ever getting this with Jonathan, so I feel grateful to still be able to have it for myself with someone else.

Different people for different needs. Not better, just different.

Driving home, I find myself lost in a daydream, imagining what it would be like to be pregnant, to have Patrick's baby, to have that bond with him. It's not possible—he's had a vasectomy, I've got my implant, and I'm sure I don't want a baby, but I think maybe I do want something like that to bond us together, something that says I'm his and he's mine. All I have is his snuggly jumper, still not returned from our forest date, but I don't feel like I can wear that when I'm with Jonathan. I push my thumb into the shell in my pocket and find some comfort in it.

Then I realise I'm missing the point. I'm not his, and he's not mine. We are our own people; we don't belong to anyone else.

My phone pings with a text from Amy: *How was your weekend with Patrick?*

For once, it's me leaving a message unanswered. I've forgiven her and I'm glad she's remembered this was a big weekend for me, but I'm still a bit annoyed with her and I like having this little bit of power over her, making her sweat a bit.

As soon as I get home, I tell Jonathan about not using a condom. Honesty is the best policy. I reassure him I can't be pregnant and I'll get an STI test, and that I've learned my lesson and won't do it again. He listens quietly and calmly, but his breathing becomes noticeably shallower, his nostrils flaring. I know I've screwed up and I'm sorry about it, but I think his anger is unfair when I'm taking responsibility for my actions.

"Is this you trying to get back at me for Amy?" he sneers at me.

What the hell? "Of course not! It was an accident. We got carried away, that's all."

He shakes his head. "You keep getting carried away, though, don't you? First with Lucy, now with Patrick. I need to know I can trust you to stay within our boundaries, or this is never going to work."

His words hit me hard, like a hand squeezing at my stomach. I'm angry at myself for fucking up like this, ruining things for myself. "You're right. I'm really sorry. I wish I could take it back, but I can't. And I'm going to deal with it straight away to put your mind at ease, I promise."

He closes his eyes for an agonising second before giving a sharp nod. He takes a deep breath. "Okay. These things happen. I forgive you, but we're not having sex until you've been tested."

That's fair enough, I suppose, but I'm desperate for some lovely reconnection sex or, frankly, any kind of affection from him, so I can feel like he really forgives me and still loves me.

Out of nowhere, I finally pluck up the courage to bring up the subject I realise I've been avoiding for the last two years. "Jon, I love you and I want to be with you forever. But I don't want to get married to you or anyone else, ever. I don't want to feel like I belong to you or that you own me. I need to be my own person." Although it doesn't feel like that's been weighing on my mind, verbalising it makes me feel instantly lighter, freer.

The surprised look on his face suggests this hasn't even crossed his mind at all. "I know. Me too. Proposing just felt like the right thing to do at the time. But I don't need to get married to know you love me."

We both smile and snuggle in together, touching for the first time since I got home. It feels safe and comforting to be held by him at last.

He has a confession of his own to make. "I've been messaging Kate this weekend."

I smile at him. This is great news. I'm sure it must've been hard for Kate too, so if they can support each other, then that's perfect.

"And Sarah too—she's split up with Jack. He freaked out at seeing that message she sent me on my birthday. It made her realise how unreasonable and controlling he was being. He was starting to stop her seeing some of her other friends too."

"Shit, I hope she's okay."

"She is, or she will be now. It wasn't flirty chat with either of them, really, but it was nice."

I smile at him, feeling this must be a sign of progress and understanding on his part. Maybe this really is all going to work out just fine, after all. I want to know more, but don't want to pry or get carried away, so I hold my tongue. He'll tell me what he wants to when he's ready. I hope Sarah does come back into his life. She did him so much good, and I'm glad she's got out of what sounds like an unhealthy relationship.

My phone pings. Wendy. "Looks like you might not be the only one starting a new job. I've got an interview at the care home next week!"

"Well done. You're going to be brilliant!"

Soft hairs tickle my nose as I snuggle into his safe, familiar chest. I come up to the pillow and lie facing him, our noses touching. "Te amo," I whisper.

"Je t'aime," he whispers back, and I can hear the smile in his voice.

When we were first together and too scared to say *I love you*, we used to find other ways to say it like this. Hearing him say it now takes me back to those heady early summer days together, our whole lives ahead of us.

I fall asleep thinking about the interview, what I'll wear, what they might ask me, what it would be like to get paid to spend time doing something I genuinely love. I want to tell Patrick about it, sure he'd be proud of me, but decide against it. It would be too embarrassing to tell him and then not get the job.

Chapter 54

Jonathan and I arrive at the park for my usual birthday picnic, and we're greeted by Patrick, Kate, Ruby, and Max. Patrick gives me a hug as he hands me a wrapped present, his warm breath intoxicating on my face as he whispers in my ear that I should wait until later to open it. That hug is probably going to be as much physical affection as I can have from him here today, and I don't want to let him go. I squeeze him a little tighter before moving away to give Kate a hug too. She's wearing glasses today and looks studious and casual compared to when I met her at her house all dressed up.

Soon Lucy joins us, her hair a halo of tiny curls around her head, looking at ease with herself in a way she didn't used to. She seems happy and comfortable in jeans and a T-shirt, her signature red lips back, whereas before it seemed that she always felt the need to dress up, like she had something to prove. Hannah and Freya are both very smart in their new school uniforms, Hannah with an enormous plaster on her knee. They've been blackberry picking, big purple smiles on their faces as they hand me the bunch of wildflowers they've picked for me.

"Happy birthday," Lucy says with a smile, handing me a cake.

"I thought I'd save Jonathan a job! It's vegan, so everyone can have some."

I can't believe she even remembered that Patrick and Kate are vegan! The cake is beautiful and I'm confident it'll taste as good as it looks, but a little part of me misses my traditional Co-op coconut cake from Jonathan. Instead, he's bought me—us—entries into a half marathon next spring in Paris, something for us to work toward together, as well as a holiday to get excited about. I've decided already that I'm going to collect sponsorship for the local food bank that opened just last year; I remember what it was like to be hungry and know how much my family would've benefitted from their support when I was little.

I hug Lucy as I thank her for the cake, and as I do, she whispers in my ear, "Dave turned down the job in Dubai. We've got enough going on between us, so we're going to sort that out before making any other major life changes."

I beam at her. This news might just be my favourite birthday present ever. I don't want to pressure her into any difficult conversations about us when she's still working things out with Dave, so I'm not entirely sure how she feels about anything else happening with us, but I don't care. I just love hanging out with her, whether it's as friends or more.

As Jonathan, Patrick, and Lucy play catch with the kids, Kate and I sit under a knobbly oak tree, its leaves just starting to turn brown at their edges. We each have a slice of cake and a glass of cold white wine and are quietly watching the fluffy white clouds passing overhead: a genie coming out of its bottle, an elephant, a dolphin. A wasp inquisitively buzzes around my wine glass before moving on elsewhere. Seeing Jonathan playing so well makes me wonder if he does want his own children really, whether he's just going along with me saying I don't want them. Or maybe he doesn't want them with me.

I slump back against the solid trunk of the oak tree as my thoughts start to go down a depressing rabbit hole, wondering why he's with me at all; he doesn't want my children, he doesn't feel the same as I do about monogamy. Why are we still together? Maybe we are just too scared to be alone, after all?

But Kate pulls me out of this downward spiral with some news of her own. "I don't think Mum's got long now. She's slowed right down and hardly gets out of bed anymore. We've had to make some impossible decisions recently, but I think we've done all we can. We've even got the funeral planned out. I think she's ready, she's had enough, but Dad is a total mess. I'm not sure he'll ever be ready to say goodbye. She needs to go into a hospice really, but I don't think she can bear to leave Dad a moment sooner than she has to."

I can't believe how she's able to talk so matter-of-factly about something so hard. I'm scared my voice will break if I answer too quickly. I gently touch her forearm and give her what I hope is a reassuring smile. "I'm so sorry. It's so sad. If there's anything we can do, you know we're right here. It certainly looks like Jonathan is getting on well with your kids, so we can babysit for you at the very least."

"Thank you. And thank you for helping Patrick when I've been difficult. I know this hasn't been easy on him either, and he bears the brunt of it from me. It's just nice to be here doing something normal today. I'm desperate for a big blow-out night out, but it's impossible at the moment. I need to be with Mum and Dad, or the kids, all the time. I just want this bit to be over now."

I don't know what to say. Saying that an opportunity for a night out will come soon would also be saying that her mum will die soon. Instead, I put my arm round her and we have a little hug. "It sucks. I'm sorry."

With their kids here and being out in public, I can't be affectionate with Patrick, and the frustration of it is driving me crazy. Although I also want to touch Lucy, it somehow feels less frustrating, maybe because I've spent plenty of time with her in a nonsexual way anyway.

Throughout the afternoon, I watch all of these people I'm building new and different relationships with interacting with each other, developing new connections of their own. Seeing Kate and Jonathan chatting away together makes me smile and feel hopeful—maybe there is an attraction there, or maybe they'll be friends like he is with Sarah. Jonathan and Patrick seem to get on well too, and that makes my heart swell with joy. But watching Patrick giggling away with Lucy, his hand on her arm, hurts. It's not fair. I feel like I'm trying so hard not to show him any affection, and there the two of them are, laughing away together happily, not a care in the world.

I remind myself that Lucy is gay and isn't interested in him. I remind myself that I really like both of these people, they're good people, so why wouldn't they get on? And I remind myself that the reason they can be openly flirty with each other is because nothing is going on. They aren't trying to hide anything from their kids precisely because there's nothing to hide. I just wish I could be affectionate with them without feeling like it was something that should be hidden.

I meet Amy for cocktails later on, the first time I've seen her since the revelation about her and Jonathan. I'm a little nervous, unsure if everything has changed between us now. But after a slightly awkward initial greeting, we seem to be back to normal with no need for explanations or apologies.

She's bought me some gorgeous and extravagant bright green feathery earrings, which I love, but know I would never have chosen for myself. She knows my taste better than I do, this friend I've had forever, who's been with me through thick and thin. Amy is just as important to me as Jonathan, and I need to make the same choice to forgive her and rekindle our friendship. What happened between them was too long ago to hold on to any anger about it now.

I get home and unwrap my present from Patrick. It's a framed photo he took of me on our weekend away. The sun is behind me, putting my profile mostly in shadow, though you can see enough to know I'm smiling. A beam of sunlight shines through a gap in my hair, which glows more golden than ever. It's really beautiful, and I can hardly believe it's me.

Later that night, head slightly fuzzy, I snuggle into my warm bed with a smile, thinking back over the last year and how much has changed, the new people we've welcomed into our lives and the joy they've brought us. Jonathan has started cycling, has become less obsessive about making the house perfect, has pushed himself harder at work. I'm running a few times a week, eating better than I ever have in my life. I'm excited about my job interview next week, seeing where it might lead me. I'm excited about getting to know Patrick and Kate better, whatever that turns out to be. I've never felt closer to Mum and Dad, or to Amy, and I'm going to be there for Lucy as she faces this new chapter in her life. I can even change a tyre! And I feel closer to and happier with Jonathan than I have in years. I feel more loved and wanted than ever before.

Most of all, I'm excited because I can't even begin to imagine what my life will look like a year from now, or ten years from now. Maybe Jonathan and I will be together, maybe we'll have split up and just be friends, maybe we'll have even decided to have a baby. Patrick and Kate might still be in our lives as partners or friends, others might be, or maybe it'll just be the two of us. Who knows what we both might be doing with work, whether we'll really get into cycling and running? I'm definitely going to find a way to visit Tom in New York as soon as humanly possible, and now I've got the prospect of a new job and more income, that feels closer than it used to.

My comfortable, predictable life has gone, and I've got the uncertainty and adventure I've craved so much. I don't need a happily ever after, an ending. No-one is interested in what happens to a couple after they get married and settle down; it's boring.

"Night-night, beautiful," says Jonathan, appearing in the doorway with my coconut cake.

Acknowledgements

I'd never tried writing fiction before the pandemic; but being stuck in my house for months on end forced me to try several new hobbies and writing was the one that stuck. Writing this book and fantasising about all the fun things I could be doing if only Covid would go away was sometimes all that kept me sane. So, I'm grateful to the lockdown for giving me the time to try something new, and grateful to the act of writing itself for how much it helped my mental health at such a difficult time.

Thank you to my amazing, kind, loving husband for getting well outside of his comfort zone to allow me to explore my desires and help me become the person I am today. Thank you to my beautiful children who make my heart sing every day, I hope your lives will be abundant with love and joy.

Thank you to all of the friends who have supported me through my journey with so much love and understanding, and without any judgment. I feel incredibly lucky that there are far too many of you to name here, but you know who you are. Thank you especially to the friends who have read and supported me with this project, particularly Suze, Laura, Josie and Kerry.

Thank you to Stephen and Chelsea and the other people I have met through my own opening up journey; whether it was for a few messages, a few dates, or more, you all inspired me to stretch and be a better version of myself. A special thank you also to Tyler, whose "I come here to write" comment inspired this whole book in the first place!

Thank you to all the authors, podcasters, and influencers who are doing their bit to normalise non-monogamy and support people through difficult feelings and conversations they might not have seen played out in the mainstream. Thank you to Leanne for her support with the foreword and to Emma and Fin from Normalising Non-Monogamy - the podcast which showed me there are so many ways to do this in a happy and healthy way.

Thank you to my editor, Rhonda, who not only helped me finish this but also took me on a very real and sometimes difficult journey of self-reflection! To the coaches who encouraged and motivated me throughout the process – Ana and Des in particular. And to my proof reader April for tidying it all up.

And finally, thank you to my mum. My act of teenage rebellion was to avoid any essay subjects you could have helped me with - I needed my independence! You always said that everyone had at least one book in them, but you never got to finish yours. You'd never have believed I would've done this, and I know you'd be so proud of me. Thank you.

I hope this book will help people who are trying to better understand their own desires, or who are trying to understand a partner or friend's different relationship needs and wants. If it's helped you, I'd love to hear about it, along with any other thoughts and feedback. Please leave me a review on Goodreads or Amazon to help others find this book.

Thank you so much for reading!

CJ xx

cjalexander.co.uk

Printed in Great Britain
by Amazon

76608253R00151